A Cursed Immortal

Journey of a cursed immortal to a Superhero in Kaliyug

HIMANSHU VERMA

INDIA • SINGAPORE • MALAYSIA

ISBN 979-8-89067-880-5

ॐ नमः शिवाय

"Ashwathama Balir Vyaso Hanumanash cha Vibhishana Krupacharya cha Parashuramam Saptatah Chirjeevanam"
Ashwathama, King Bali, Ved Vyas, Hanumaan, Vibhishan, Krupacharya and Parashuram are seven death-defying personalities.

(Padma Puran - SB 8.13.12,17; Garuda Purana - 1.87.36).

Contents

Acknowledgement

||ॐ नमः शिवाय||

I dedicate this book to Lord *Shiv*.

Whenever I read this book, many times I feel how, could I write such a story, I have been writing this book since 2016, but the amount of energy, I received in April 2023 after visiting *Kedarnath Dham* was amazing. It's *Mahadev's* blessings, that I could write such an amazing story. Many times, it happened that the words, characters, their description and weapons, came to my mind, automatically and I just kept writing, it's *Baba Kedarnath's* blessings and these are his words not mine

Remembering my mother late *Shri Radha Rani Verma*

This piece of work is dedicated to my wife-*Sarika*, who was first to know, that I am going to write something, and she appreciated without delaying any second.

My cute little daughters, *Shikhi* and *Venu,* they inspire me to live more and do more for them, they give peace of mind, which enables me to do constructive work.

This book would have not been completed, without two persons, my younger brother *Shivanshu Verma*, who helped me a lot to publish this book and helped me to get creative art work for the book, whole art work is supported by him only.

Second, Dr. *Gagan Sharma*, he was my editor on spiritual aspects of the book, he helped me greatly in drafting scenes related to *Ramayan* and *Mahabharat* times, such as – The *Sudarshan Chakr* stolen by a *Rakshs* from Lord *Vishnu* and when *Hanumaan ji* stayed on earth while Lord *Ram* asked him to return to heavenly abode with him. There are many such scenes, which he helped me to define properly.

I told this story, initially to my close family members and some friends, they all appreciated it at once, that was my first motivation to make this book with best to my efforts and publish the book ASAP, I can't move forward without thanking all of them.

My Sister *Jaya*, my brother-in-law *Gulshan*, their kids *Ayush* and *Avi*. My borther's friend *Arun* and *Ankit*.

I dedicate this book to *Sadhguru Jaggi Vasudev*, he is my first *Guru* on spiritual path, there are lot of references and inspirations from him in this book, though it's an original work, I am obliged to *Sadhguru* for his directions and inspiration to write such content. I never met him to learn in person, just saw him from distance in two events, no direct interaction, but that is not required even in today's time, social media is enough to interact and learn from distance, I can say I am his *Eklvay*, he taught me great lessons of life, he taught me, how to think, how to handle life situations, how to live and how to bow down to Lord *Shiv*.

I am inspired from many great personalities born on this earth starting from *Adiyogi Shiv* to Lord *Ram*, Lord *Krishna, Mahaguru Chankya, Swami Ramkrishn Paramhans, Swami Vivekananad, Mahaavtar Babaji*, our beloved Prime

Minister *Sh Narendra Modi*, HH *Shri Shri Ravi Shankar, Devdutt Pattnaik, Amish Tripathi*, Dan Brown, Jim Carry, *Jiddu Krishna Murthy, Osho, Uday lal Pai* and my close friend Victor *Ghoshe.* Victor *Ghoshe* is a famous author, many years back he gave me direction to read right books and to select good subjects and writers.

Many more such people taught me, many great lessons of life, which gave me strength, knowledge, and skills to write this book. I am thankful to all of them and all those whom, I missed to mention here, my humble apologies.

Preface

Dear Readers –

I can vouch, that this book is different among all stories written on *Ashwathama* till date. You will feel while reading first chapter, that this is same repeated story narrated on *Ashwathama* multiple times, that he is alive since past 7500 years, and spotted in one or another temple.

This is not true for this book, I must admit, It is every writer's compulsion, that if we want to narrate any story on *Ashwathama*, we have to go on late evening of *Mahabharat's* 18th day of war, without going there, it is difficult to know the cause, how that great warrior, son of *Guru Dron* and Lord *Shiv's, Rudr* incarnation steeped so low that he projected *Brahmastr* on *Uttara's* womb to kill an unborn child.

I started this book in the year 2016, I wanted to present *Ashwathama* as a superhero of *Kaliyug,* but one thing never digested me, that how a person could survive in such a bad condition for last 7500 years. As per my limited knowledge even a person in healthy body, cannot live for 7500 years in same body.

That's why it took me many years to understand, how a cursed *Chiranjeevi,* whose body is full of wounds, who is suffering from leprosy, bleeding continuously from his forehead, is living in physical form for 7500 years. Above that, he is spotted by many people, worshiping in one or another temple, this never digested me.

These two things are contradictory, he is either suffering from leprosy and must be wandering somewhere for treatment, and must be in such a condition that, he will not be even, able to walk few steps, but if he is seen worshiping in temples then, there must be some improvements taking place in him, which means curse of *Krishna* is fading somewhere.

Maybe I am wrong, my limited knowledge is not capable to take me beyond this understanding, but as an ordinary person, what I do not understand, what I cannot justify myself, I cannot even dare to put it in front of my readers.

It took me many years to understand, multi layered dimensions of the body and life, to understand this, I did not only read spiritual books but also read Einstein, Stephen Hawking, Fritjof Capra and many other scientists to understand, what is the structure of the universe and what is life and death.

By the end of the year 2022, I got some facts, understood some principles, which can stand true on both scientific and spiritual scale. Found answers to some questions which can be understood on all the three levels of modern science, Indian Vedic science, and spirituality.

That's why I request, instead of making your opinion on this book, on first chapter, wait till third chapter. I look forward to your questions, arguments and look forward to your queries. I can be contacted through: -

hverma2506@icloud.com

I request all the readers, if you want to read a different story about *Ashwathama*, then read the first chapter only as base of this story. I can guarantee, that by the end of the second chapter, you will realize that, this is not same old story, narrated multiple times, where people still see *Ashwathama* bleeding from the forehead, living in physical form for 7500 years with a diseased body.

||ॐ नमः शिवाय||

Chapter 1

The Great Mahabharat War

5500 Years BC, Dvapara Yug

Battlefield of *Kurukshetr,* Late evening, 18th day of war. *Bheem* smashed *Duryodhan's* both thighs in the Mace dual. *Duryodhan* was lying on the ground, his both thigh's femur bones ruptured and dislocated from pelvis.

Ashwathama, *Kripacharya* and *Kritvarma* and *Duryodhana's* eldest son *Durjay* are only warriors left in *Kaurav Sena.*

Pandav's didn't had any personal grudge with left out four warriors, so they left them and declared their victory in Great *Mahabharat* war.

But *Ashwathama* is raged in anger, he couldn't handle [1]*Adharm* done by *Pandavs.*

- *Bheem* attacked *Duryodhan* below the waist, which was not allowed in Mace dual.
- *Yudhishthir* lied to *Guru Dron* for *Ashwathama's* death, saying truth so low, that he could not listen.
- *Dhrishtdyumn* beheaded *Guru Dron,* when he laid down his weapons, deboarded from his Chariot and sat

---

[1] Here *Dharm* and *Adharm* doesn't translate to English literal meaning, *Dharm* means duty, duty for nation (*Rashtr Dharm*), duty as son (*Putr Dharm*), duty for society (*Samajik Dharm*)

in mourn, for fake death news of his son *Ashwathama,* while closing his eyes in mid of the battle field.

- *Arjun* killed *Karn,* while he was weapon less and was pulling his chariot, steeped into the mud.

Ashwathama came to *Duryodhan* and promised him, I will take back *Hastinapur* tonight, war is still not over, I can lead *Kauravs* whatever is left.

Duryodhan is happy to see, there is still hope left in his army, he asked a pot of water from the river.

Durjay brought the pot, *Duryodhan* announced. *Ashwathama* as Army chief of *Kauravs* and honoured him with water *Tilak* on *Ashwathama's* forehead, Gem was shining on *Ashwathama's* forehead, which gave one more hope to *Duryodhan* to win the lost war.

Kripacharya, Maternal Uncle of *Ashwathama* asked, how you are going to win the war, we *Kauravs* can be counted on finger, and *Pandavs* are still there in huge number.

Ashwathama pointed towards an owl, who killed many sleeping crows on trees.

Kripacharya screamed, are you mad, killing warriors after sunset, while they are sleeping, is not *Dharm.*

You have been with *Duryodhan* since your youth, but still you have never been blamed for any *Adharm* done by *Duryodhan,* either it was *Draupadi's Vastr Haran*, or *Laaksha Greh* conspiracy, or any other misdeed done by *Kauravs,* you were always away, and your image is still of a great warrior who follows *Dharm.*

Duryodhan was raged to hear this and *Ashwathama* was surprised, it was first time his *Mama Kripacharya* praised him so much.

Ashwathama hopped on his chariot and moved towards *Pandava's* camp, saying, was it *Dharm,* when they brought a woman *Shikhandi* to kill, *Pitamah Bhishm.*

The rest had no way, except to follow their commander so, *Kripacharya, Kratvarma* and *Durjay* followed *Ashwathama,* towards *Pandav's* camp.

Tonight, something happened, which never happened in whole war time of 18 days, *Ashwathama's* sword was swirling like blood monger monster, he killed everyone came on his path in *Pandav's* tent.

His *Satv Gun* neutralised and *Tamo Gun* was at peek and *Rajasv Gun* was somewhere lost, that's why he lost sense, who is coming in front, children, women, old person, any one he saw, he just killed.

He entered *Dhrishtdyumn's* tent, *Dhrishtdyumn* heard the voices, he was ready to fight, but he was not able to face *Ashwathama* even for a second, *Ashwathama* beheaded him the way he killed his father.

The whole cosmos runs on three Gun or qualities- Rajo Gun, Satv Gun and Tamo Gun. For example, our food is also categorised as Rajsik, Tamsik and Satvik. Similarly, each specie is categorised in these three qualities. Trees and Plants are considered as Tamsik Yoni, because they cannot move, whereas human life is considered Satvik form.

Nothing is bad or good, all three are inherent qualities that balances the nature. Sleep is also considered Tamsik but sleep is not bad, it requires body to rejuvenate while sleeping, our body repairs, while sleeping.

Every being's thoughts and actions are also categorised in these three qualities, which changes as per time, thoughts or our company with others.
Beings, act as per their balance, as of now Ashwathama was full of Tamo Gun so he was acting like one.

Dhrishtdyumn's brother *Yudhamanyu* came to rescue, but he was also not able to face even first strike of *Ashwathama.*

Then he ran towards *Pandav's* tent, where all five were sleeping, he beheaded all five in one sword.

Ashwathama picked five *Pandav's* heads and ran towards *Duryodhan.*

Uncounted soldiers, women, children who so ever came close to *Ashwathama's* path, sacrificed to *Ashwathama's* anger, rage and vengeance, the land was filled with blood and flesh. The night was so fierce full, looks like Lord *Shiv* came in *Ashwathama's* body to play dance of destruction, like *Maa Kaali* came herself with a skull in hand to kill every *Pandav* and drink their blood.

Whoever were able to escape, *Kripacharya, Kritvarma* and *Durjay* were there to kill them.

They shielded *Ashwathama's* path towards *Duryodhan* and continued killing everyone in *Pandav's* camp.

Once *Ashwathama* went far ahead of *Pandav's* camp, they also followed him.

Ashwathama reached *Duryodhan* and screamed, *Duryodhan* hold your breath friend, your enemy's head is in my hand, you won this war, don't die my friend.

Duryodhan heard the scream, he could not believe, what his whole army was not able to do, What *Pitamah*

Bhishm and *Karn* was not able to do, *Ashwathama* did with 3 soldiers in few hours.

When *Ashwathama* stopped at *Duryodhan*, he showed 5 *Pandav* heads, *Duryodhan* asked to give *Bheem's* head in his hands.

Ashwathama hanged heaviest head towards *Duryodhan*, *Duryodhan* crushed it in a second with his hands, while lying on ground.

He screamed, no this is not *Bheem*. This soft head cannot be *Bheem*.

Kripacharya, *Kritvarma* and *Durjay* followed *Ashwathama*. When *Kripacharya* heard *Duryodhan's* scream, he checked all 4 heads, they were not *Pandavs*, they were teen kids who looked like *Pandavs*.

They were 5 sons of *Draupadi- Prativindhya, Sutsom, Shatanik, ShrutKarm* and *Shrutkirti*.

Duryodhan screamed, now *Kauravs* will kill innocent children to win war and he took his last breath.

In a while *Bheem* came, followed by *Arjun, Nakul, Sehdev* and *Sri Krishna* himself.

Krishna came with his active *Sudarshan Chakr* in his finger, as *Ashwathama* saw it, his discussion with *Krishna* before the war in *Dwarka* flash backs, when he requested to acquire *Sudarshan Chakr* and *Krishna* said that, only *Brahmastr* could face *Sudarshan Chakr*.

Ashwathama was not in his senses, only *Brahmastr* was echoing in his mind. He invoked *Brahmastr*, when *Arjun* saw this, he had no other option except invoking another one to counter *Ashwathama's* attack.

Suddenly the atmosphere changed, birds and animals started crying and roaring, they started running here and there.

Big cyclones started taking form, loud thunders bolted in the sky, sky turned totally dark.

Krishna took back his *Sudarshan Chakr* and screamed *Arjun,* to take back his *Brahmastr* as well, *Arjun* understood the intensity, so he called back, but *Ashwathama* could not, because he never learnt how to recall *Brahmastr*, he thought something and diverted it towards, *Uttara's* womb to finish *Pandav's* last hope of lineage.

Ashwathama already killed their five sons, now he tried to finish *Pandav* clan completely by killing last descendent of *Pandav* clan.

Early morning, sun was about to rise, dance of destruction stopped, *Krishna* roared on *Ashwathama.*

You have committed unforgivable sin, you attacked unborn child in Uttara's womb, this is worst of worst sin, you fired Brahmastr on a pregnant woman, last hope of Pandav's and last hope of Dharm. And before that you killed Draupadi's five teen sons, while they were sleeping, how low will you go Ashwathama. You are son of Guru Dron, Rudr Incarnation of Lord Shiv.

Krishna- I can kill you immediately, but I respect *Brahma Ji's Chiranjeevi* boon over you, so I curse you, that you will live till eternity as per *Brahma ji,* but you will be attacked by worst of worst diseases.

(*Krishna* in his fiercest form), I curse you *Ashwathama* that your body will be infected with leprosy, from this time onwards, till you live on this earth, every pore of your skin will secrete peep instead of sweat. You will smell so badly that nobody will ever dare to come near you, you will forget all your knowledge and your *Dhanush* (Bow) will never come back to you.

Kaliyug is about to start, due to the effect of *Kaliyug,* people will fight for every small thing, people will become more selfish and greedy, and in such a time, a person like you with such bad condition, will have to face worst of worse situation, humiliation will be at par.

You will plead for death, but you will get only suffering and nothing else and every suffering will remind you of the grave sin you committed. You will set an example to everyone, what happens if we break boundaries of *Dharm,* what happens when a pregnant woman is attacked, what to face if an unborn child is killed intentionally in the womb.

The world will remember you *Ashwathama* but only as sinister, a monster, a malefic son, **A cursed** *Chiranjeevi.*

Ashwathama in remorse broke down, the monster in him soaked in blood vanished, he cried in remorse- *Oh god,* what I have done, I am no less than a monster.

He knelt on his knees and bows down to *Krishna's* feet, hey *Vasudev kshama kshama,* I want to die kill me, kill me now. I am not worth standing on earth, even for a single moment. I should offer myself to *Agni dev* to clean my soul.

I have done, what should have not been even thought off, I was frustrated, I lost everyone, my father, my friend *Duryodhan* everyone, *Pandav* killed my father with trick. *Kaurav's clan* is also finished, I was in fiercest anger.

Krishna (cooling down)- I don't interfere in nature's rules, you have committed worst sin and like all others, you have to face the results, you take it or not, it's your *Karm,* you have to pay for your *Karm*. For the tricks and cheat done by *Pandav's* they will pay for their *Karm*, you don't have to think about their *Karm*. Anyway, you finished their progeny, what else you want to do with them now?

Krishna while leaving- You must wait *Ashwathama*, there is no shortcut, finish your *Prarabdh Karm* of this life before *Nirvan*.

You tried to end *Pandu* lineage, to balance out your sins you must pay, more to the cosmos than you did.

Krishna and *Pandavs* left the battlefield, to see *Uttara's* unborn child.

Ashwathama was still there, bowing down on his knees, as he was on *Krishna's* feet, but *Krishna* was not there, he left.

Ashwathama cried and cried out loud like horse, this was the second time when he cried like a horse[2]. As he cried, peep started coming out from his body, he was feeling powerless, bad smell touched his nostrils, he thought its dead bodies, whose smell is spread everywhere in the battlefield, so he tried to run out of the battlefield, but to his surprise he could not stand up, he was limping. He again tried to stand with all his will power, he wanted to get rid of this foul smell, the smell of Gemstone (*Mani*) which use to give him ecstasy on his forehead (*Ashwathama-Mani*) is lost. *Krishna* took the *Ashwathama-Mani* and left a wound on his forehead.

Ashwathama started moving with his limped body, his childhood memories started flashing out in his eyes,

[2] When *Ashwathama* was born, unlike normal children, he cried like a horse, that's why *Guru Drona* named him *Ashwathama*.

when he used to jump and run like a young horse, *Dron* his father used to smile on his boyhood activities, his father loved him a lot, but today he is confused, was it my father's unconditional love, which brought me to this situation, My father used to play many tricks while teaching with *Kauravs* to give me extra knowledge, he always favored me most, till *Arjun* came in his life. He asked immortality from *Brahma ji* for me.

Was I, a good student and a son? was it company of *Adharmi Kauravs* which brought me to this situation?

Ashwathama questioned himself- who is reason for this situation, did *Krishna* wanted me to get into this situation or was it, *Duryodhan*? *Ashwathama* was trapped in his thoughts and continuously moving when something suddenly took him out of his past.

Eish this bloody smell, his body odor started increasing at fast pace, he stopped and looked back, there were no dead bodies, *Kurukshetr* was left far behind, he couldn't imagine how far he came from the battlefield.

Hours passed, it was bright day, Sun was on head, though there was no one visible, all were sacrificed to great *Mahabharat* war, those who were left, *Ashwathama* killed last night. There was no house left, barren land visible as far as he can see.

Ashwathama found a pond and moved ahead to quench his thirst, his image was visible in the water, as he saw, he broke down, he screamed from his lungs, this is not possible, this cannot be *Ashwathama,* dull burned skin, bumped face, he realised this foul smell was his own, his hands were shivering due to paralysis. He forgot to drink water, kept crying and crying, sitting on the bank of pond.

After some time, this diseased figure sprawled unconscious on the pond side.

Few hours later, third phase of day reached, sun was about to set, *Ashwathama* woke up, hungry, thirsty, tired and infected, he checked his body, smell was still there, wounds were increasing, he drank some water, ate some fruits which fell from the tree nearby and again collected his will power and started searching for holy river *Ganga,* he was sure, as he will take one dip in holy river *Ganga,* his lovely figure will again appear, it's just 18 day's dirt of war and nothing else, *Maa Ganga* is great ancestor of *Kauravs,* she will cure me definitely. *Ashwathama* moved towards Ganga.

CHAPTER 2

The Markandey Clan

Kaliyug, Year 2016

Markandey clan, descendants of great sage, *Rishi Markandey*, the clan is ardently dedicated to Lord *Shiv* and *Shiv* family for many 1000 years.

People in this clan lives very simple life, they meditate, learn Sanskrit literature, do physical exercise and pranayama to go deeper into *Yog*.

Children in the clan use to learn *Shiv Stutis*, *Shiv Sutr* and *Shiv Puran* by heart at very tender age, every child knows minimum three languages, *Hindi, English* and *Sanskrit*. Every person in this clan, can easily communicate in all three languages.

That's not the only identity of this clan, all these people don't live in villages only, neither all are saints only, they all are well educated people and are into mainstream of today's life, working on higher posts or having great business across the globe.

The whole community is well educated and spread across the world, in different streams of work, some dedicated their life to mythological era of India, many became Archeologist, book writers, University professors and research scholars, and many are priests in many reputed temples of Lord *Shiv* across the globe.

This clan is so dedicated to Lord *Shiv* that, in the history of this clan, as people remember, there was no marriage outside the clan, neither the younger ones had ever tried so, not because of caste difference but due to love and dedication to Lord *Shiv.*

They believed that a girl from another family may not have the level of dedication to Lord *Shiv,* as they need in this tradition, so a woman from other tradition, caste or sect may not understand their tradition and love for Lord *Shiv.* So, they prefer marriages only with in the clan.

This way, they also kept their genetic pattern intact for generations.

Many people conducted research about this community, to understand their root of success, why there is no poor in the community, why everyone is so cool and calm by nature and physically fit, how everyone has some work to do, and not sitting idle in name of Lord *Shiv*.

No one has ever seen any *Markandeyi* to show off, they can live in big houses, can own big cars, still behave like common person and live simple life, In spite of having so much wealth and knowledge. Infact, many of them are at very prestigious positions. Many of them own big businesses, people dream to work in their offices, because working in their company is best experience, employees are well taken care, work-life balance is maintained at highest level.

Those who are in jobs, they are most humble people, companies grow if there is one *Markandeyi* working in the company, still they do not fight for salary raise or promotion.

Researchers say that the reason behind their success lies in sheer devotion to Lord *Shiv*, meditation and *Yog*. *Yog* is first thing every child learn along with *Shiv Puran*, during their childhood, that's why they are intact from greed or any other worldly desire. Everyone in the clan try to reach higher level of consciousness and that's what they are taught by their parents, from the day, any child starts listening or understanding.

There is a believe that, if 2-3 *Markandey* families lives in any community, the society feels a greater change in terms of positive energy and social issues, like clean roads and walls. Violence and theft decreases drastically. Every family in such locality reports greater changes in them, personally and mentally.

Like every *Shiv* devotee, Non-dualism is only philosophy. These people also believe in *Aham Brahmo Asmi* (I am universal consciousness).

They believe everything is part of them and they are part of everything. They don't ignore issues, infact gets into action, wherever required, try to resolve the issue. This clan is very much self-reliant and understand their responsibility towards society (*Samajik Dharm*), nature (*Prakriti Dharm*), country (*Rashtra Dharm*).

One of such family member, in this clan is – *Uma,* she is M.Sc. in Mathematics, and was a visiting professor in many universities nearby to teach Algebra and trigonometry while she was in *Chennai.*

Mahesh, her husband was a quantum physics scientist, worked in CERN, Switzerland. She chose housewife role, after giving birth to *Samikshit*, her lone son. One of uncle of *Mahesh* was in Bali, Indonesia as Chief priest in Lord *Shiv* temple.

Uma's father *Shiv Charan* was Fighter pilot in Indian Air Force and served his life during 1972 war.

6 months back *Mahesh* died in a car accident in Switzerland in suspicious conditions, the police reported that his car got uncontrolled and slipped in deep valley.

No one in the clan including *Uma* believed, because a *Shiv* devotee like *Mahesh*, never drive rash, neither they get into any wrong company, nor break any rules.

few months earlier, *Mahesh's* Uncle in Bali, Indonesia, also reported to be dead, due to heart attack.

Many such suspicious deaths occurred in this family and in this clan, in last 1 to 1.5 years, every death happened mysteriously, the count of death was exponentially increasing in the clan, only few families and persons were alive.

Many people from other clan believed that since they are very old clan and don't marry in other clans, they are being cursed by *Mahadev* himself, or may be their DNA is deteriorating. Many people, many theories, everyone was projecting their own ideas behind these deaths.

Markendeyi were disturbed, no men or women in the family died a normal death from last 1.5 years, all died in suspicious way, but there was no evidence of any kind of murder, or attack. Police and Medical reports used to be very clean and shows only natural death.

Uma and many others members of this clan, who were left in very small number, were disturbed and fearful, they had intuition that someone is behind them to finish this clan. *Uma* now had her only son *Samikshit* left in the family.

Almost 5 months back, all those, who were left including *Uma*, gathered in village *Kaithi*, Varanasi, to meet *Guru Aksi* and consult on series of events happening in this family for last 1 - 1.5 years.

Kaithi is main clan village of *Markandeyis*, in this village, Lord *Shiv* came himself to save their *Kulpita, Rishi Markandeyi*.

Guru Aksi was Head of the village *Kaithi* and Spiritual *Guru* as well for all the villagers and *Markandey* clan. All *Markandeyis* used to consult first, *Guru Aksi* in any situation.

Guru Aksi is a young-looking person at age of 50, he had a different shine and calmness on his face.

Heavily built body and good height, simple grey hairs, his brown eyes can attract anyone in first glimpse.

He looked like a warrior Yogi, who has attained peace and non-violence for the sake of his people. he used to wear simple payjama and kurta mostly made of khadi or cotton having one front pocket, always keeping a diary and Bhairavi Yantra in it, he wears simple sandals made of leathers mostly in design of lion skin, This sandal was his only passion as per the villagers, no one had idea from where he gets such sandals, there is no single pair available in whole Varanasi.

Guru Aksi already had some idea about all these issues, and he was working on these mysterious deaths for last 6 months, something he came to knew, which he can't explain to everyone as of now, so he suggested everyone to settle in unknown locations, for some time and he will get back to everyone in right time.

Guru Aksi was more concerned for *Samikshit*, because he knew, that if there is anyone who can save this clan, then it is only *Samikshit*. That's why he suggested *Uma* to move towards *Yamunotri* and settle in *Purali* village. Which is also one of the *Markandeyi* village and many people of this clan still live there, but not known to the world. Both *Uma* and *Samikshit* were living in disguise, in *Purali* for last 6 months.

Samikshit was a teen boy, soon going to be turned 16, on next day of coming *Maha-Shivaratri* and an amazing devotee to Lord *Shiv*, his traits were exceptional in *Shiv* devotion. There was no scripture left, he hadn't studied on Lord *Shiv*. His *Yog* skills and meditation capacities were amazing, people saw that when he used to meditate, he always rises a little bit above from the ground. As per the community, *Samikshit* never meditated on the ground, he always floats while meditating. They used to compare *Samikshit* with their *Kulpita* (Father of the clan) *Markandey*.

Samikshit similar to his family lineage, was very well learned boy, he knows by heart every, *Shiv-Purana*, *Shiv Stuti*, many *Strot, Mantr and Shloks.*

His mother tongue is *Tamil,* and he has full command over *Sanskrit, Hindi* and *English* even he was learning some foreign languages. He wanted to further spread *Shiv Yog* in many parts of the world, that was his plan for his career, though destiny planned something else for him.

CHAPTER 3

Samikshit

Kaliyug, 5th Mar 2016

***Yamunotri* is one of the *Chhota* (Mini) *Char-Dham* in Uttarakhand, which is also origin of River *Yamuna*.**

There is one village *Purali* in *Yamunotri* range, famous for *Markandey Purana,* written by *Rishi Markandey* (founder of this Shaivait clan aka *Markandey* clan). A small number of families used to live here, most of them belonged to *Markandey* clan, while some were followers of this clan and ardent *Shiv* devotee.

Uma settled here six months back, after losing everyone in the family and on *Guru Aksi's* suggestion, to keep safe, her only son *Samikshit.*

It was almost 6 months when *Uma* settled here, she kept herself busy in household, and society work, while *Samikshit* joined a *Gurukul* in nearby area. *Uma* initiated a Self-Help Group to generate some income, though income was not an issue for her, since her family left good wealth and pensions for her.

But this [3]SHG was helping other needy women in the village, who have no business for 6 months during winters,

[3] Self Help Group

they use what they earn in summers, it also keeps her busy. Tourist season was about to start in month of April. *Uma* planned to get good income for every village woman.

Yamunotri is in valley of *Himalaya*, that's why here days are smaller, evening starts at 5 pm sometimes even 4 pm, that's why people close, daily work early and sleep earlier.

Today as usual *Uma* started sleeping at 8 PM, she was totally tired of daily work and slept in deep sleep, as she closed her eyes, she heard some whispers in her ears. "Leave this place with *Samikshit* and go some safe place". She was getting this voice for last one week, but she ignored it every time, thinking it's her illusion, she became overprotective for *Samikshit.* Because anyway death incidences decreased in last 6 months, after meeting *Guru Aksi*. Nothing seems dangerous.

She again tried to ignore, but today the voice was quite strong and fearful, she could see a blurred semi human figure who was jolting her to leave. She immediately woke up, totally wet in sweat, her throat was dry. The figure was still there, clearly visible to *Uma*, he again said, leave *Uma* leave, as soon as possible.

Uma can't believe, what she saw in dream was in real, looks like *Ashtwakra* was right, when he said in [4]*Ashtwakra Geeta* that whole cosmos is a bigger dream.

This is not normal, *Uma* sensed, it's some divine soul who cares for her family, it was not possible to ignore now, she already lost everyone.

---

[4] *Ashtwakra* was royal purohit for King *Janak*, father of *Ma Sita*. He explained that whole cosmos is a big dream in *Ashtwakra Gita*.

She decided to leave, she woke up *Samikshit*, took some money and clothes and quietly slipped away, in the night. *Samikshit* couldn't comprehend, why she wants to leave in the night, but he stayed with her without saying anything, it was not his nature to question elders.

Just few steps away on the bus stand, a Local Jeep came to get passengers for *Dehradun*. Both hopped on it, it was around 4-5 hours of journey by local transport, due to night, route was almost empty, so they reached early, it was her first time in *Dehradun* and she had no contact here, so they planned to go towards Railway Station.

In whole journey she was thinking of that divine soul who came to her. On the other hand, *Samikshit* was also puzzled.

On Platform-1, *Kumbh* Express was standing, due to two hours late arrival, both hopped in General compartment, without ticket. They didn't purchased ticket, neither *Uma* tried to get it, she didn't want to lose last transportation from this unknown city.

Both hailed lord *Shiv* and boarded the train. Due to March month general compartment was almost empty, both decided to sit on upper birth, as they moved upside, Whistle blew, and train left the platform.

Samikshit asked, where are we heading, *Uma* signaled him not to speak and told him to cover with quilt and sleep. *Samikshit* saw fear in *Uma*, he understood some problem is there, he took the quilt and slept quietly.

Uma was lost in her thoughts, who was this divine soul, why he was so concerned for us, what was about to happen in *Purali*. Is there something bigger than my perspective, which I am not able to comprehend. *Guru Aksi* had some information, but he didn't said anything, just suggested everyone to live in disguise and unknown locations. Don't know what he did or what was the solution but at least, his suggestion was working till date.

Thinking all this, she even didn't knew when she gone in deep sleep.

When *Uma* woke up, it was already morning, there were only few people in the compartment, some people were ready to deboard, she enquired which train is this, one co-passenger mentioned its *Kumbh* express, and *Lucknow* station is going, he deboarded while saying so.

She again asked someone, while coming down from upper birth, which will be the next station. One passenger replied, *Sultanpur* is next big station and then it will end at *Varanasi*.

Uma knew only few places in North India, But *Varanasi* is the word which gives her immense peace. Almost 6 months back, she was here, to meet *Guru Aksi*. She decided to deboard at *Varanasi* and called *Samikshit* down as well from upper birth. She took her phone to calculate ticket cost and penalty, but phone was dead. *Samikshit* never carried phone.

In few hours, *Varanasi* station arrived, she took some money in hand and moved towards station exit.

She thanked Lord *Shiv*, because knowingly or unknowingly *Mahadev* brought her to *Varanasi*.

Kaithi Village of *Varanasi* is their ancestral village, where their father of this clan, *Rishi Markandey* was saved by none other than Lord *Shiv* by *Yam*. She was feeling safe here.

The train was late by 4 hours, it was almost 5 PM, when train finally ended at *Varanasi* station. She held *Samikshit's* hand tightly, deboarded the train and ran towards the exit, to reach *Kaithi*.

6th March 2016, Evening 6 PM

Almost 6 months back she was here, she remembered road to her village and that home as well, where she wanted to reach.

She was making it fast to reach, as well as keeping low profile and hidden, not to be identified by anyone, *Uma* was worried, don't know, who is attacking her family and clan and may be, still someone following her. Fear and quest both were overpowering her.

Once reached *Kaithi* village, she moved towards a particular house, the house of *Guru Aksi*. It was already around 6.30 pm in the evening.

Uma rang the bell, but no one came, she feared even more. She prayed for everyone's wellbeing and entered the house and called *Guru Aksi* with fear- *Guru Ji*.... *Guru Ji*....

Everyone in the family were busy in evening *pooja* with *Guru Aksi*, *Guru Aksi's* wife *Ganga* came to see, who is calling *Guru Aksi* so passionately. When she saw *Uma*, she was surprised to see her, till then *Guru Aksi's* daughter *Shreshtha* also came there.

While seeing everyone in evening *Pooja*, *Uma* also bowed down to *Mahadev*. Finishing *Pooja*, *Guru Aksi* also came to *Uma* and asked with heavy tone, so finally you reached safely.

Uma was surprised, because *Guru Aksi* was not surprised, even for a second, for *Uma* and *Samikshit's* arrival in *Kaithi*, though *Guru Aksi's* whole family were happy to see them.

Samikshit also bowed down to Lord *Shiv*, then bowed down to *Guru Aksi* and greeted everyone in the family.

Ganga and *Shreshtha* brought tea and snacks, whole family surrounded and asked about what happened to them, how they came here, without any information, where they were for last 6 months?

Uma told *Guru* and the family, that on *Guru Aksi's* instruction we shifted to *Purali* and I am coming from there only. As everybody heard *Purali*, all were shocked.

Till then many other neighbours came to see who has barged in *Guru Aksi's* home.

This is identity of Indian villages, guests come to one home, but whole village gets information.

Uma was confused, why everyone's face is so pale, *Guru Aksi* understood and without saying anything, he opened the TV, switched to news channel. Continuous news was flashing on every news channel, about disaster happened in *Purali* Village.

The news was showing that- a big part of mountain sledged and the whole *Purali* village swapped away. Teacup dropped from Uma's hand, Samikshit also shocked to see, they were not able to express their feelings, should they be happy, or cry for Purali Village.

Everyone had only one question to *Uma* and *Samikshit*, how on earth, they escaped this disaster. Since last night whole *Kaithi* village is trying to connect to *Purali*, but no one is picking up. Even *Uma's* phone was not reachable.

Purali village is well known to Guru Aksi and the villagers of Kaithi, both villages are interconnected because of Kulpita Markandey. Kaithi was the place where Lord Shiv saved Rishi Markandey and in Purali, Rishi Markandey wrote Markandey Puran. That's why both the villages are mostly inhabited by Markandeyis only and connected to each other, some had family relations as well.

When Purali villagers come for any work or ritual in Varanasi, they stay in Kaithi and while doing Chaar Dham Yatra by Kaithi villagers, they used to stay in Purali. Many Purali villagers come during their last time in Kaithi to attain death in Kashi.

Due to this continuous movement, both villages, made beautiful guest houses in both villages.

Uma told whole incidence, what happened to her last night. Everyone understood that this is not a natural disaster. Fear was now at its peak, their enemy was no longer killing one by one, now he was destroying entire villages.

Everyone had many questions in their mind, some wanted to ask *Uma* and some wanted to ask *Guru Aksi*.

> *There is strong believe that, the one who attains death in Kashi, attains Nirvan (free from cycle of death and birth). There are many Mukti Dham or last time shelters in Kashi, where people in their last time comes to stay, the rooms are given maximum for 3 months, if the person doesn't attain death, then he or she need to leave.*
> *If we see spiritually, there is no need of relatives and people of acquaintance at the time of death, because the presence*

of any close person and expressing their grief, makes it more difficult for the soul to leave the body, that is why, if we see closely, every religion or sect's last time rituals are made in such a way that it helps the soul to separate from the body and ensure that the soul does not try to enter again in that dead body. Hindu rituals are full of such activities like, tying up both the toes of the foot, shedding ashes in flowing water etc etc.

In Vedic times of Mahabharat and Ramayan, there are many such incidences where even kings left palaces in last time and moved to Jungle, this last stage of life is called Vaanprasth Ashram (Move to the Jungles). In Mahabharat, Dhritrashtr along with Gandhari and Kunti also left to Jungle to attain death after the war. Surviving in jungle for few days is fine, but living for a longer period is not possible, for people now a days, May be coming to Kashi in last time, now a days is a form of Vaanprasth Ashram.

Every *Kaithi* villager was watching same news, on TV and Mobile on *Purali* for last one day.

The news was devastating, nothing left in the village. For *Kaithi* people it was like their second home is gone with all relatives, they were in extreme shock and anger.

Guru Aksi said, I know everyone has lot of questions, we need each other's support and suggestions, so let us sit tonight after dinner and discuss.

Guru Aksi already invited whole village in the morning, for tonight's feast.

Guru Aksi said, that lets sit tonight after dinner and pray for peace of every departed soul in *Purali* and then also discuss on other things, including preparation for *Maha-Shivaratri*.

According to Vedic scriptures- The fourteenth day of every lunar month or the day, before the new moon is known as Shivratri. Among all the twelve Shivratris that occur in a year, Mahashivratri, the one that occurs in February-March month is of the most spiritual significance. On this night, the northern hemisphere of the planet is in upward position, and there is an upsurge of energy from the core of the earth towards the sky.

On this night, if we sit or stand straight, this energy will pass on through our body, aligning our Chakr, and help to open Sahasrar Chakr in just one night of meditation. The usefulness of this night is equal to many years of meditation. On the other hand, if we lie down on this night, then we obstruct this energy path, which creates disturbance in our body's energy balance.

Einstein and Stephen Hawking, understood that everything comes from nothing and goes back to nothing.

Stephen Hawking mentioned in his one the book- 'Brief Answers to the big questions'- The Universe is the ultimate free lunch, means it is created out of nothing.

Shi (That)-Va (Not) means Nothing, That's why in Hindu tradition, Shiva is notion for endless emptiness of the cosmos and this vast nothingness is called Shiva.

It is in this context that Shiva, the vast emptiness or nothingness, is referred to as the great lord, or Mahadev.

On this Maha-Shivaratri, Saadhu, Sages and Shiv devotee sit or stand whole night and try to be part of this vast nothingness and encourage others to sit whole night as well.

By evening, all villagers gathered in temple area. The food was brought in temple area, *Guru Aksi's* family and other ladies helped in preparing.

Guru Aksi first offered food to Lord *Shiv* and then *Prasad* was served to all villagers.

A big feast organized that night in the village, after a long time.

After dinner they sat in open space. Bone-fire lit in the center. *Guru Aksi* was sitting on his *Aasan,* made of cement in temple ground and people sat surrounding him. Everyone was sitting in calm posture but there is only one curiosity in everyone, what is this all going on, why this disaster occurred in *Purali*, what is going to happen next?

Uma explained everything, what happened to her in *Purali*, what she saw in dream, all thanked Lord that some divine soul came at right time to save her and *Samikshit*, but the devastation jolted everyone.

Guru Aksi asked villager to volunteer for re-habilitation of *Purali* village, all were emotionally attached to *Purali* village, almost 70% of the villagers were willing to go to *Purali,* for rehabilitation and rescue work.

He also asked *Uma* and *Samikshit,* if they would like to volunteer, but *Uma* was still in dilemma, she was not getting answers to her quest. She again pressed same question to *Guru Aksi*.

Who was that divine soul? And how this disaster happened in *Purali*? Almost everyone in the village also eager to know, that how this disaster happened.

Guru Aksi again quietly addressed the village, there is time for everything, and I believe this is not right time neither right place.

Uma was little furious, *Guru* I lost everyone in the family, there was big attack on our village, and we were saved somehow, when the right time will come, after we all are killed by this unknown demon force?

Guru Aksi calmly asked, do you fear of death, do you think death is the end, is this what you have learnt in all years of *Shiv* Devotion.

Uma realised her mistake.

I am sorry *Guru,* I am not worried about my death, I am concerned for my son, and people of this clan. Should we leave this problem as it is and wait for the murderer to come here and kill all of us, because we are not afraid of death, because we will be again born as Shaivaits.

Isn't it our *Dharm,* to save our people and kill the devil.

Guru Aksi said, *Putri* you have already contributed to this war, you have given birth to a child, who will be our savior and savior of this clan, don't worry about him, *Mahadev* is with us.

War?

This word jolted everyone; all faces looked towards *Guru Aksi.*

Guru Aksi understood, he uttered wrong word in wrong time. This is not right time to explain the real cause, he kept quiet and wait for others to keep calm. When he saw everyone is quiet and calm, he again said, there are many things, I need to explain to all of you and we need to do many things as well.

The next morning of *Maha-Shivaratri*, we all will leave this village, some of us will leave to *Khandwa, Madhya Pradesh* and some of us will leave to *Purali, Yamunotri*.

Uma asked - you mean *Asirgarh* fort[5]?

Guru Aksi said- yes *Putri*, *Asirgarh* fort, help is waiting there for all of us. *Bhima* is on the way; he is coming with some Jeeps to take us there.

Uma asked in astonishment - who is *Bhima*. You said WAR, which war you are talking about?

Guru Aksi smilingly said- The time is coming *Putri*, tough time is gone, its just matter of few more hours, we have solution to the problem. As of now I am not in situation to tell you everything, neither this place, nor this time is right.

All I can assure you that, we are not alone and solution to our problem is also very close.

Just wait for few more hours, before leaving we need to do lot of work tomorrow, you all have faith, Lord is with us. As of now, let's finish what we need to do- we need to do *Shradh Tarpan* for *Purali* village, prepare for *Maha-Shivaratri*, then wake up whole night and then we need to leave this village.

I request everyone, to take some rest tonight, its already too late and we have to pack, to leave this village, we all will be waking whole night again tomorrow to discuss further.

Guru Aksi continued, so we will be separated in two teams, one team will go to *Purali* for rehabilitation of the

[5] A fort built by King *Asa Ahir* in early 15th Century, in *Khandwa* district, *Madhya Pradesh* presently.

village and find out if anyone is left. I announce my son, *Ajay* as the group leader for *Purali.*

Rest of us will leave for *Madhya Pradesh* with *Bhima.*

Uma asked once again- okay but at least you can tell me about that subtle figure which I saw.

Guru Aksi replied, he is a great soul and now onwards he will be your *Guru.*

Many people in the village whispered- **our** *Guru,* **our** *Guru.*

Guru Aksi requested everyone to keep quiet and go to their homes and prepare. We are left with very less time.

Samikshit felt uneasiness and he asked to *Guru,* are you going somewhere, are you leaving us?

Guru Aksi smilingly said- *Guru* never goes my child, I will always be there.

While leaving, *Guru Aksi* came close to *Uma* and said, the divine soul which you saw and *Bhima* both are going to help us together, they are related.

Some people were still there, *Uma* and *Samikshit* moved to village Guest House.

One person immediately moved to his home, locked his room and rang a number on his phone.

Uma and *Samikshit* went to their rooms, villagers also moved to their respective homes, but some words kept rolling in everybody's mind, tonight all were lying on their beds, but nobody was sleeping.

Words by *Guru* Aski were echoing in every ear.

War, *Guru Aksi* is leaving, *Bhima, Asirgarh* fort.

Everyone got some sense, that there is something in *Purali* which can be danger to us, and this danger is still there, anything can happen to us. No one still got clear picture, whether it is a disease, which is killing all of us or there is some enemy or a group against us?

Whoever it is, how on earth someone can move a mountain to finish a village or is it really Lord *Shiv,* who is furious on us, if it is Lord *Shiv's* wrath then, why *Guru Aksi* said, War?

Uma was even confused, the subtle form I saw is related to *Bhima*, who is *Bhima*, who that subtle form could be? How come that divine soul knew about disaster in *Purali*, and may be on his orders *Bhima* is coming here to take us from here, means, we are still in danger in this village, is something about to happen here as well?

In other words, *Guru Aksi* has ordered whole village to evacuate, this even jolted her badly, she hailed Lord *Shiv* and tried to sleep, she can't comprehend any more.

***

In the morning, the whole village woke up early 4 am in the morning, there were lot of things to be done, due to *Purali* disaster, nobody could prepare for *Maha-Shivaratri* for last 2 days. Anyway no one slept properly last night.

Now they had to offer *Shradh-tarpan* of *Purali* villagers, who were massacred by an unknown devil and after that they need to prepare for *Maha-Shivaratri*, and then all had to leave their *Kaithi* village.

Guru Aksi made a team of young Shaivaits in the village, who used to go nearby villages and invoke everyone to wake up whole night on *Maha-Shivaratri*. He also used to conduct some sessions for people who don't understand the scientific significance of *Maha-Shivaratri*.

> *It is believed, that sleeping or lying down on the night of Maha-Shivratri is physically the biggest loss for oneself, and one who sits or stands on this night, without doing any worship or work, gets great results, that's why Guru Aksi tried to ensure that on this night, no person should lie down, irrespective of religion or sect. It has nothing to do with religion or sect. It is a natural phenomenon, which can, either be of great benefit or harm.*

In the morning everyone gathered at the place of worship, The atmosphere was very serious.

Guru Aksi came with smiling face, his face was bright, Guru Aksi's family members and villagers were surprised, in such a tensed moment, how come, Guru Aksi could be so happy, what is the reason?

Guru Aksi saw all awkward faces and he understood, He said, tomorrow, Samikshit will be 16 years, and that is the day, I was waiting, from tomorrow onwards, our problems will be over, our saviour will rise to save us.

He again smilingly invited everyone, to start today's activities.

Havan was organized, *Guru Aksi* did collective *atm-shuddhi Havan* for all deceased people of *Purali* and then collective *shraddh tarpan* conducted.

The young Shaivaits team left for nearby villages, *Guru Aksi* had full day, scheduled for orientation session on *Maha-Shivaratri* for foreign visitors in *Kashi* and many online sessions.

Uma tried to connect *Guru Aksi,* she was now more eager to talk to him, but he was busy from one session to another, and she could not get time till evening.

It was evening, all occupied in *Maha-Shivaratri poojan*, everyone wanted to invoke Lord *Shiv* as per their own way. All were loaded with lot of queries, fear, doubts and questions. Someone was unhappy to know that they have to leave the village, don't know for how long or will they be able to come back or not, where some were totally focused to worship Lord *Shiv*. Some were lost in *Guru Aksi's* words.

Guru Aksi, alerted everyone to start the *poojan*, he called *Samikshit* and asked smilingly, now you are our saviour, so you take the lead and start the *pooja*.

Samikshit wholeheartedly abided his *Guru*, he sat on prayer bench in right posture, spine very straight, chest puffed up, sober face, breathe in rhythm, it seems as if a Commander is getting ready for war. Then the auspicious sound of *Nirvan Shatakam*[6] started, reverberating in the atmosphere.

मनोबुद्धयहंकारचित्तानि नाहम् न च श्रोत्र जिह्वे न च घ्राण नेत्रे
न च व्योम भूमिर्न तेजो न वायु: चिदानन्द रूप: शिवोऽहम् शिवोऽहम् ॥1॥

Today there was a different aggressiveness in the village, seems like they all wanted to talk to Lord *Shiv* right now, why this is happening, why this clan is on verge of extinction. Why this devastation happened in *Purali*, is there a bigger danger on us?

While one young man *Prakash*, who was quite angry with all the incidences, he started singing *Shiv Tandav Strotam* in front of *Agni Kund.*

जटाटवीगलज्जलप्रवाहपावितस्थले
गलेऽवलम्ब्य लम्बितां भुजङ्गतुङ्गमालिकाम् ।
डमड्डमड्डमड्डमन्निनादवड्डमर्वयं
चकार चण्डताण्डवं तनोतु नः शिवः शिवम् ॥१॥

Uma planned to chant *Shiv Chalisa* whole night, without eating or drinking anything.

दोहा
जय गणेश गिरिजा सुवन,
मंगल मूल सुजान।
कहत अयोध्यादास तुम,
देहु अभय वरदान ॥

6 A six-verse composition in *Sanskrit*, made by *Adi Guru Shankaracharya* at age of 10, which summarises the basic teaching of Non-duality.

चौपाई

जय गिरिजा पति दीन दयाला।
सदा करत सन्तन प्रतिपाला॥

She wanted to invoke Lord *Shiv* to come and rescue her son, *Samikshit*, like he came many 1000 years back in this village, to save father of our clan, *Rishi Markandey*.

Guru Aksi decided to chant *Mahamrityumjaya Mantr* for whole night, to save whole clan, whoever are left out now in any part of the world.

ॐ हौं जूं सः ॐ भूर्भुवः स्वः ॐ त्र्यम्बकं यजामहे सुगन्धिं पुष्टिवर्धनम् उर्वारुकमिव बन्धनान्मृत्योर्मुक्षीय मामृतात् ॐ स्वः भुवः भूः ॐ सः जूं हौं ॐ।

It is said that, if you are still part of one Gotr or clan and never altered your DNA code in your genes by marrying in another Gotr like what this Markandey clan has done, then people of whole clan can be connected at genetic level, or we can say that, their energies can be found at same frequency, just like a radio channel can be heard or catch by any radio on one frequency, from any place. Similarly, children of same clan, can be benefited if something is done at frequency that matches particular Gotr.

Energy can be transformed to all under same genetic code, (that is the reason many clans still worship their Kuldevta first before any ceremony), one prayer or Anushthan done in one place, will benefit everyone of this clan, living in any part of the world, because they all are connected with same genetic memory. Their 'Çhitt' is connected to some extent, Guru Aksi wanted, that everyone in the clan, to feel safe and be alerted of any danger.

The human genome is organized into 22 pairs of autosomes and one pair of gender chromosomes. Where both parents contribute one chromosome for each pair. The X and Y chromosomes, known as the gender chromosomes, determine the biological gender of child: female child (XX genotype) inherits X chromosome from the father, Male child (XY genotype) inherits Y chromosome from the father. Mothers contributes only X chromosomes. The presence or absence of the Y chromosome from father determines gender of the offspring, **not the mother**.
We can say that Gotr is 'Y' Chromosome of our DNA helix. Which is present in same code in whole clan if it is intact.

The whole village kept awake and prayed for whole night, in one or another way.

***

This morning brought a ray of hope in everyone. No one knew how the night passed, while everyone was very tired, no one had slept properly, the night before, and everyone was working hard during the day. The sorrow of *Purali* village, was doubly affecting everyone's heart. But this morning must be a new opportunity for Markandeyis.

Pooja completed at 6.05 AM, *Prasad* distributed to everyone, while some people turned towards *Guru Aksi,* he slumped on his right side, everybody rushed to him, as some people came close to *Guru Aksi* he was gone.

Everyone was shocked, he is not so weak that he could not stand, two nights without sleeping or one whole night *Pooja.*

Prakash immediately caught him, he was completely lifeless, *Prakash* placed his head in his lap and checked his pulse, nothing was left, *Guru Aksi* was no more.

As soon, tears welled up in *Prakash's* eyes, *Uma* understood that it is an attack, she ran towards *Samikshit* in panic. *Ajay* also realized that a great crisis surrounded them, he immediately cordoned off, *Uma* and *Samikshit* with two more persons.

Two more people *Rudr* and *Jogi* along with *Ajay* ran towards the forest with *Uma* and *Samikshit.*

CHAPTER 4

Another Massacre

In the village, the villagers gathered *Guru Aksi.*

Prakash the angry man, checked *Guru Aksi,* but no bullet, no arrow, nothing was found on his body, he checked his pulse, and it was confirmed *Guru Aksi* is no more, somehow while raising *Guru Aksi's* head on his lap, he felt something on his neck, it was very small invisible sharp arrow in shape of a needle, *Prakash* sensed the attack and screamed to **run, run away**, but before they all could move, there was dead silence in the village.

In a moment, all 40-50 people were dead. All were injected with same poisonous needle; the poison was so strong that no one was able to move even a little bit.

Suddenly a figure came out- *6.2 Feet height, black cargo, black T-Shirt, black high boots, head covered with black scarf, one end of scarf, used to cover his face.*

There was a shining armor, covering his back till waist, he clicked a button on his armor belt and a metallic black plate in shape of 20 inch measuring scale, popped up from his armor, he pulled a lock on the plate, suddenly multiple plates of same size started sliding one by one in circle and converted into a round shield, he chanted some *Mantr* and all the needles poked in the villager's body, pulled back and sticked to the shield. Looks like all needles were magnetically charged and could be called back after the attack.

The figure checked some people randomly, for any sign of attack or wound but, successfully there was no sign of any wound. Then he checked specially, all teenage boy's faces and captured every teenage boy face in his mobile.

Finally, he poured some special ash in the *Agni Kund* and left the place.

Asirgarh Fort

Ajay, *Rudr* and *Jogi*, guarding *Uma* and *Samikshit*, were running in the jungle, *Ajay* was in dilemma his family was there in the village, but his father's order last night compelled him to be with *Samikshit.*

They were only 1 kilometer away from the village, while a jeep came at lightning speed towards them and stopped forcefully, just before hitting anyone, sound of breaks could be heard at distance, driver screamed, **hop on..., hop on......** The driver in jeep was about to touch *Ajay* with his Jeep, who was running ahead of everyone.

The Jeep came so fast, *Uma's* heart stopped beating, she thought now it's end of everyone, all were feeling same, they are now surrounded by enemies completely.

Then the voice came, I am *Bhima.* He smiled and greeted everyone.

This name gave them a great relief. They all boarded the Jeep without any delay. *Bhima* greeted with *Om Namah Shivay* and introduced himself- I am also from *Markandey* clan, don't worry, I will be taking you to safe place and then he just drove out of the place immediately, saying nothing he just focused on driving faster and faster. *Ajay* said- *Bhima*, I am son of *Guru Aksi*, he told us about you. Are you also *Markandeyi?*

Uma also added her question, do you know what happened in *Kaithi* village?

Bhima replied, yes, I am also son of *Markandey* clan, though we live in separate place.

Bhima – I request not to think what happened to *Guru Aksi* and the village, I request just take some rest, our prime focus as of now is to leave this place safely, as soon as possible. At this moment, *Samikshit's* safety is our priority.

I request, that you all take some rest and let me drive, we need to move fast, and we need to be safe as well.

Bhima's reply was not satisfactory, it generated more tension for everybody, they sensed there is something wrong at gross level.

Ajay was disturbed, he didn't know what happened to his father, his family, infact the whole village. There was no call from the village, he was also not able to make any call, there was no network. All what happened in last 48 hours, about *Purali* village devastation and then this attack, started flashing in front of him.

His father, *Guru Aksi* started behaving strange, since past some days, he made all calls in private, though generally he used to talk on speaker phone. His meditation time increased. He started giving responsibilities to everyone and instruction, specially to *Ajay*.

The day *Uma* came, he announced a feast for whole village, even before *Uma* knocked our doors. What he knew, what he was hiding. *Ajay* was totally confused, was *Guru Aksi* already knew, his death is coming, so that he arranged- **The last supper**.

He first ordered, in front of all villagers that, I will lead *Purali* team and then in person he told me to take care of *Samikshit*, because he knew the danger, and with *Samikshit* my chance of survival is more than going to *Purali*.

Ajay's head started rolling, in a moment he went to deep sleep.

The last supper

A very famous last supper happened in history, which was conducted by Jesus Christ on his last night. Leonardo da Vinci's famous portrait of Last Supper is worldwide famous for various reasons and a great work of art.

This is old tradition in Indian system, when a Yogi or Sadhu knows he is leaving or plan for Samadhi, a supper is organized by him/her before leaving the world, those who goes unaware, the family conducts the supper on 13th day, named as Tehravi.

Uma who was also tired but had not enough courage to sit awake, all memories rolled from the day, she saw a soul in her dream while in *Purali*, to her travel to *Kaithi*, *Maha-Shivaratri* and then *Guru Aksi* and now in this Jeep, what's going on, is there some big force, who wants to end our clan or only my son.

Why I got this dream, while in *Purali*, who was that divine soul, she was lost in her own thoughts, *Uma* also felt her head is rolling and she also went in deep sleep, while the jeep was continuously crossing from one place to another.

Likewise, one by one all went to deep sleep, *Samikshit* took it long to sleep, though he was also disturbed from last 3-4 nights. *Bhima* was surprised to see inner strength of *Samikshit*, but he kept silent and kept driving.

***

After many hours of travel, the jeep halted in a small village in jungle near *Narmada* River. It was dark, everyone suddenly woke up as the breaks screeched, *Uma* was unconscious, but as the Jeep halted, she screamed, Where have you brought us?

All woke up on *Uma's* scream, some villagers also came near Jeep to welcome the guests. *Bhima* folded his hands and explained to *Uma*, it's my village *Nandpuri*, near river *Narmada*, Its *Khandwa* district in *Madhya Pradesh*.

Khandwa, reminded everyone of *Guru Aksi*, and felt safe, they are in right place.

It was almost midnight, *Bhima* covered 20 hours journey in just 15 hours.

Everyone was asleep in the Jeep, during whole journey except *Bhima*, still everyone's head was aching.

Bhima was also tired but still politely said, don't worry *Maa,* we are in safe place, it's my village, *Markandeyi* village. This is the place where all your questions will be answered, I would request first to settle down, we have arranged rooms for all of you, just relax and settle down. There are lot of things we need to discuss, its better all of you, reenergize and then we talk in the morning.

This village is also *Shiv Devotee's* village, and some people belongs to your clan, I am also from same clan, so nothing to worry, take rest for the night and then we will meet tomorrow morning to discuss and plan next course of action.

All were still in trance, they were not able to comprehend anything, still *Uma* murmured, *Shiv* devotees, what kind of *Shiv* devotees, there is no sign of Lord *Shiv* anywhere, only *Krishna* idols and *Vishnu* idols are visible everywhere.

Some people came and took *Ajay* in a separate room, *Rudr* and *Jogi* in a separate room and *Uma* and *Samikshit* in one room.

They had no choice, all were relentlessly tired, they were in a different village, a different city, and a different state altogether. These people don't seem to be dangerous, but they are not *Markandeyi,* that *Uma* was sure.

The place and the bed were very comfortable, food and water were served in the room to everyone, but as *Uma* touched the bed, she fell asleep, so did everyone else, no one even dared to drink a glass of water.

CHAPTER 5

Bhima's Truth

As the Sun started rising, birds started chirping, this noise was enough for *Uma* to wake up, at same time *Samikshit* woke up, both were feeling fine now, they got ready as soon as possible.

As they came out, *Bhima* came to them, greeted and asked them to come to his place and have breakfast.

Till then *Ajay*, *Rudr* and *Jogi* also came out from their respective rooms.

Bhima was taking everyone to the courtyard of his house. in between many villagers were coming in the village from outside having, chalks, paint buckets, paint brushes and many other such things.

Damayanti, *Bhima's* wife was waiting for all guests with *Jalebi, Poha* and Tea, she greeted all guests.

Uma greeted *Damayanti* and asked *Bhima,* are these people coming from some work in the night.

Bhima said while sitting on the chair, let's have breakfast first, while sipping tea and said, all of them had left here at night, on my orders. All of them went to write the name of Lord *Ram* in 5-kilometer radius of the village.

Uma asked, is this some kind of tradition, and asked while sipping tea, taking a pinch, you all are devotees of Lord *Shiv*, then why the name of Lord *Ram*?

Bhima understood, he has been caught.

He stood up, bowed his head with folded hands and said, forgive me all of you, I have told many lies.

- *First of all, I am sorry that I dosed you all yesterday in the Jeep with anesthetic gas, so that, you all sleep easily and let me take you to this place, I am extremely sorry but I felt this was the only way, to bring you all safely to such a remote place and let me drive for a such a long journey without any hassle.*
- *I am not from the Markandey clan, I just said to gain your trust, so that you all sit in the Jeep, I am neither a Shaivait, I am Vaishnav and this whole village is Vaishnav and devotee of Lord Krishna.*
- *Third thing, Ram Naam was for the protection of all of us from the danger, Markandeyi clan is facing right now.*

Ajay angrily replied, my father yesterday told us about you, that's why we hopped in your jeep, I wish, you would have given us time to explain.

Bhima said, I'm sorry, I didn't had any alternative than this, but I have to admit that you all are very high level seekers, no one slept easily, this anesthetic gas effects for 20 hours on 50 people in one spray.

Ajay asked, but why you were not affected with the same gas.

Bhima replied smilingly with folded hands, because this gas doesn't affect some of the genes including me.

Uma exclaimed that's why my head was aching badly since yesterday, inspite of sleeping whole time in jeep, I again slept in your guest house, without eating anything.

Though I sensed when I landed here, that this is not a Shaivait village, but I was not able to resist.

Bhima, still standing with folded hands, apologized again.

We live here to serve Lord *Krishn* and since we are not Shaivaits, we have no danger what, whole *Markandey* clan is facing.

Bhima still standing with folded hands.

Uma and *Ajay* were calmed to see *Bhima* so apologetic and said let's discuss further, whatever happened is wish of *Mahadev*.

Ajay while sipping tea asked, what was this *Ram* name in 5 kilometers of radius.

Bhima, was concerned for breakfast, he requested everyone, to take some food.

All were too hungry, they hadn't ate for many hours, all finished *poha* in 5 minutes. It was amazingly delicious.

Bhima finished his tea and started explaining, while we landed here last night, I instructed my best people, to write *Ram* name everywhere on the outskirts of the village, in 5 km of radius.

Because what I am going to tell you now, is not an ordinary enemy, nor is it a short story, you all have a hearty breakfast, the story will go on for a long time.

Jalebi fell out of *Ajay's* hand; what does it mean he is not an ordinary enemy?

What happened in *Kaithi* yesterday, he asked and took out his phone, but battery was dead, everyone else's phone was also switched off.

Bhima called his daughter, *Subhadra*, and put everyone's phones on charging.

Till now everyone had eaten something or the other, *Bhima* was waiting for this moment.

I know you're about to call in *Kaithi*, but it's of no use now, there's no one there anymore, *Bhima* said and switched TV and turned-on News Channel.

Everyone was shocked.

Ajay asked what it means, that my father is no more. In the meanwhile, news of *Kaithi* village started flashing on the news channel, stating that-

Some Castor plants fell in the fire pit (Agni Kund) in famous village Kaithi of Varanasi, which caused sudden death of villagers instantaneously on auspicious night of Maha-Shivaratri.

Uma shouted, what is she saying, poisonous gas. Everyone has gone out of their senses, someone destroys the whole village and these people can't see the real attack.

There was no limit to the grief of *Ajay* and the rest of *Markandeyis*, *Ajay's* doubts were over now, it was clear that his father knew everything.

Entire *Nandpuri* village gathered there in no time.

Everyone together consoled *Ajay*, *Samikshit* and the rest of *Markandeyis*.

Ajay said crying, while sitting in the Jeep yesterday, I realized that my father was no more, and he probably knew all this beforehand, so he had asked all of us to leave *Kaithi* village, but by then it was probably too late. Everything is over, nothing is left.

Bhima hugs *Ajay* and says, a lot is left my friend, and a lot has to be saved. Many people of your village have survived who were already sent by *Guru Aksi* to the nearby villages for *Maha-Shivratri*.

Uma asked what is left now and we, who are not able to save our clan, how will we save this world or anyone else as a matter of fact?

Bhima consoled everyone, you all have to have courage, it's tough time, we need to prove ourselves, we all are with you.

Bhima continued, the story is long, and time is short. If you all listen to me, then I will answer all your questions, who is our enemy and how *Samikshit* will save us from all this mayhem.

Water offered to everyone, *Bhima* was also emotional, everyone in the village were sad.

He started again, whether we are *Shiv* devotees or *Vishnu* devotees, its order of our Lords that, no matter what the situation may be, we should not lose our patience. We are among the best devotees in the world, we must follow our Lords. Today, it's not mere coincidence that Shaivaits come here in the house of *Vaishnavs*, this is a message to the world, that Shaivaits and *Vaishnavs* are not enemies, On the contrary when these two different schools meet, they can win the world.

After listening to *Bhima's* words, everyone calmed down a bit, and *Bhima* continued further.

A living being is composition of many bodies- the physical body or Gross body (*Annmay kosh*), the subtle body (*Sukshm Sharir*), the energetic body (*Karan Sharir*) and conscious body (*Maha karan Sharir*).

Out of 25 components, 18 belongs to Subtle bodies while only 5 belongs to the Gross body.

Where *Sukshm Sharir* has some main component- *Mann*, *Chitt*, *Budhhi* and *Ahamkar*, 7 energy *Chakr* and

3 *Naadi- Ida, Pingla* and *Sushumna* and many other components like, *Gyanendri* (subtle form of knowledge i.e; hearing, tasting, seeing, touch and smelling).

Buddhi (Wisdom or conscious mind) is our controller, which guides us to take decision, which helps us to discriminate, discrimination in sense of discrimination in good or bad, right or wrong, likes and dislikes.

We believe whatever we do, we do it because of our brain or mind (Conscious Mind), but Buddhi (Conscious Mind) is not independent, it is under influence of Mann (sub-Conscious Mind). Whatever our Buddhi decides, it is under influence of Mann.

Our mind says, we should study, so that we can earn money, but it is our sub-conscious mind, who wants luxury and brain discriminates, that luxury comes from money, and money comes from Job or Business, which needs education, so our brain inspires to study, and we believe it is our brain, but the cause is sub-conscious mind not conscious mind.

But Mann (sub-Conscious Mind) is also not independent, it is under influence of Chitt (Un-conscious mind). Chitt is warehouse of memories of many past lives, which drives Mann to think in one or another way.

That's why we have seen that, many people are not after money from birth, irrespective of the family they took birth, rich or poor. Every being born is bound with one or another habit from birth. Twins, born from same parents, brought up in same environment, but still, they may have different habits and nature, because it's not Genes, neither parents hereditary character, which is reason of

our nature, it's our Chitt, a warehouse of memories of past lives.
The fourth component is Ahamkar, it's also not in its literal meaning, Ahamkar means, knowledge of self, such as- I am man, I am Human Being, I am Indian, I am father, I am mother, I am rich etc etc.

Uma interrupted and said, we know about Subtle body and whole this anatomy, who better than a *Shiv* devotee can know about Subtle body, Our *Adiyogi* is first *Yogi* who transcended to *Nirmankaya* and still available to us in Subtle body from many thousand years.
In our clan a 5-year-old child knows about it.

Nirmankaya, is one of the forms of Samadhi, where a Yogi leaves his physical body and lives in subtle form. He uses Sadhna to make Subtle body so gross that it can be visible in some span of time, like once in 100 years, 1000 years and infact 10,000 years.
It is believed that Lord Shiv and Lord Hanuman attained form of Nirmankaya and that's why they are visible even till today on some occasions and perform some work.
Hanuman Ji came to Goswami Tulsidas, when he was writing Ram Charitmanas.
Hanuman Ji also came in Dvapar Yug and met Arjun first and then helped him in whole war.
These Nirmankayas are in subtle states, they live in a very minimal way. They choose to be in that state, either out of their compassion, or they have been ordained.

Adiyogi who first understood and cracked Yoga, he chose to sustain the longest period and hence he resides in very subtle form.

Hanuman Ji had to be Nirmankaya, because Lord Ram told him to be so, to sustain Dharm in the world, and he will be on Earth willingly, till Ram name is chanted on this land.

Bhima felt his mistake, he apologised I am sorry, I forgot whom I am talking to (smilingly). Ok let's come straight to the point, *Samikshit* smiled, yes that's better way.

Bhima started – You know who *Sunira* was?

Uma said yes, I know about him and the *Sukshm Sharir* he created, which is still not manifested in human form.

He wanted to create another *Adiyogi*.

Bhima smiled- Yes you are very correct, *Sunira* was not able to manifest a full *Sukshm Sharir*, though there were many other great *Yogi*, who could do this at very ease, such as *Ram, Krishna, Brahma, Vishnu, Hanuman* and many more such great *Yogis* in the past, but everyone has not done this knowingly.

About 35,000 years ago, there was a Yogi called Sunira. This Yogi tried to consecrate a being. The idea was to create an ideal being, who can transform the whole world in a positive way. This being reached a level to get full form. Many other Yogis have put their inputs into this being. Bhagwan Gautam Buddh mentioned about Sunira. Though the complete transformation never happened, Sunira could never get into complete form.

Bhima continued, but there was an egoistic *Tantric*, highly knowledgeable *Rakshas* King and great *Shiv* devotee, 85,000 years back, who manifested a full active Subtle body.

Samikshit asked, whom you are talking about, is there another Lord *Shiv*.

Bhima replied, no Son, not another *Shiv*, but with grace of Lord *Shiv*, about 85000 years back, his ardent devotee was able to consecrate a subtle body.

This great king was *Raavan* and the Subtle body he created was *Adhira*.

Almost whole village was there, by now, everyone was eager to know everything.

Adhira..... Adhira.......

The only word, echoing in whole village.

Bhima saw the eagerness, so he continued the story.

Discussion to be continued.........

CHAPTER 6

Adhira

85000 Years ago, Treta Yuga

After abduction of *Ma Sita*, *Raavan* was tensed, he knew that abduction of *Sita* may cause great disaster, He had idea that he could be killed, he checked his horoscope himself, and called many scholars to check, *Shani* effect on him.

He found everywhere that, his death is inevitable, no one to tell him that, he would be victorious.

Raavan was very proud of himself that, no man on this earth, could defeat him, so even after knowing all this, he did not returned *Sita Ji*, but he got engaged in a task, that if he really died, then, he should sustain on this earth in one or another way.

He vowed that he would establish a subtle body, which would be consecrated, without help of any existing soul and subtle body of any living being. His *Mann* and *Chitt* will be totally clean and under control of *Raavan*. The *Chitt* of that subtle body will be as *Raavan* wanted to inscribe, so that the subtle body will act as per *Raavan* wish, till he will exist on this earth, he will establish *Raavan's* name and continue *Raavan's* reign.

This subtle body will be so powerful, that it will sometimes appear in physical form and perform some acts, as per *Raavan* wishes.

Raavan called his brother *Ahiraavan*, who was a great scholar of *Bhairavi Tantra*, he captured many ghosts, witches and vampires for *Raavan*, to follow *Raavan's* instructions.

Ahiraavan said that all the souls and subtle bodies you want, will be at your feet, but it is not in the capacity of anyone except *Mahadev*, to create a subtle body without any dead person.

It is even more impossible when this work has to be done in a limited time period, you want it to be ready before the war, it is impossible.

Lets understand someone wants to raise a mountain, he or she needs rocks and soil to raise it, he will dig earth and collect rocks from other place to raise the mountain, so eventually there will be a cavity in the earth, parallel to mountain. The mountain is erected and negative mountain is that cavity made out of digging. This is also known as anti-matter theory, if a matter is made, it is made by anti-matter and that's why anti-matter is called God Particle *in physics.*

If Raavan needs to erect a subtle body out of nobody, he needs to gather Mann, Chitt, Buddhi and Ahamkar from somewhere else, in this matter it's a difficult task, it's not soil he collects and build a mountain. He would require same God-Particle, which creates any matter, to create a subtle form, that's why it was difficult task.

By the way there are two cavities near Mount Kailash, one is known as Mansarovar Jheel and another known as Rakshas Taal.

He prayed *Adiyogi Shiv* to get help, but *Adiyogi* never came to help him, *Raavan* understood, *Adiyogi* was furious because of abduction of *Sita.*

Without wasting any time, he started the work, for this he sent *Meghnath* to all the three *Lok* to get high class *Tantrik* and *Yogi* who know anything about subtle body.

Raavan also called his 9 dear *Yogi* brothers, who were more than *Raavan's* life to himself, *Raavan* assigned them to control his 9 qualities. 9 *Gun* namely Lust, Anger, Greed, Attachment, Malice, Hatred, Partiality, Adultery and Cheating.

He kept the tenth quality, Ego, with himself to manage.

For this work, a *Yagya Shala* was prepared in *Lanka,* which was magnificent to see and was built with completely scientific approach.

A hall almost 2500 Sq ft in size, height more than 40 feet, black painted walls from inside. On the north-west direction there was a rock seat in design of lotus flower established, 3 feet high above the ground, encircled with reflecting glasses from all sides, creating a cylindrical shape, except 4 feet space in front open, so that the Praan Shakti (Life energy) transformed by Yogi, concentrates on the lotus seat, due to reflection on all sides, making a 360° revolution of energy on the lotus flower rock seat, which will increase day by day.

A big Agni Kund was placed in front of this rock seat where 15 Yogi could easily sit to perform Yagna.

Raavan started the process to consecrate the subtle body and announced to offer his and his 9 brother *Yogi's* head to Lord *Shiv* in this very *Agni Kund.*

He called *Meghnath,* his beloved son to add high amount of *Akaash Tatv*, the power of *Akaash* (Ether) element which *Meghnath* had mastered.

He also called *Kumbhkaran*, his younger brother to give earth element (*Prithvi Tatv*), as he had mastered, earth element by eating continuously for 6 months. This earth element will be used to make physical features for this subtle body.

Our body is composition of 5 elements- Water (72%), Fire (4%), Earth (12%), Air (6%) and Ether (6%) known as Panchbutas or Panchtatv, any physical form is combination and balance of these five elements. These Panchtatvs are required for a physical body not for a subtle body, but Raavan wanted something in between, so he wanted more of Akaash (Ether) Tatv from Meghnath. Raavan used Earth element from Kumbhkaran for physical features and Ether element to combine all physical and subtle matters in one form.

All 9 brother *Yogi*, *Meghnath*, *Kumbhakaran*, *Ahiraavan* and *Raavan* himself, locked themselves in *Yagya Shala* with an objective, either there will be a Subtle body or there will be no one, they will offer themselves to Lord *Shiv*.

In the first month, the first *Yogi* i.e. *Kama Yogi* sat and presided over the *Yagya*.

As soon as the *Yagya* started, thousands of souls and subtle bodies filled with *Sanchit Karm* started hovering in the *Yagya* hall, *Ahiraavan's* job was to keep away any such beings who have *Sanchit Karm*.

Agni Kund continued with pious fire, unstopped and the powers of the first *Yogi* in lead, was getting weak day by day, by the end of the first month, body of the first *Yogi* i.e. *Kama Yogi* was left with only a skeleton of bones, on the other side something started to deepen in the lotus place.

30 days passed it was time for the second *Yogi* i.e. *Krodh Yogi* to take the lead. Night of thirtieth day was about to over, sun could rise any time.

Kama Yogi recited the gross body displacement *mantr*, raised a sword and his head fell into the fire pit. The rest of the body also disappeared. The sword fell there, some water appeared at the *Yogi's* place and some soil, the rest of the air and sky elements merged in the *Yagya Shala* environment. There was nothing left that needed to be cremated, the gross body made of five elements merged into five elements.

Those who attain Samadhi, no cremation rituals are required for them, because cremation rituals are meant to disconnect Soul with the body, so that the Soul understands, that my relation with this body and relatives of this body is over and he or she needs to take next birth. New birth, new body and new Karms.

In Samadhi, the Soul knowingly leaves the body, in complete consciousness, hence the Soul does not fight to come back to body, so there is no chance, that Soul will try to enter the body, that's why no cremation rituals are required. Infact there is high amount of positive energy felt near the Samadhi area, which can benefit those who visits.

On the other hand, there are even next level Yogi, who knows how to dismantle the physical body which is made of Panchtatvs- Water, Fire, Air, Earth and Ether. This is next level Samadhi, where Soul leaves the body and while ejecting, body itself dissolves into Panchtatvs and nothing is left to perform last rituals or even establish the physical body as Samadhi or Mummy.

We have heard, people had skills to disappear and go some other place or appear after some time, in same place. But this is not disappearance, they dissolve their body in the cosmos, no chance to come back at all.

We have two examples of such great Yogi in present time. Ramalinga Adigal a Tamil saint, who locked himself in a room, on 30th January 1874 and when the door was opened nothing was found.

Saint Kabir of 15th century, who chose Magahar, near Gorakhpur for his death, which was declared as most unsuspicious place, to attain death by many scholar Brahmins of that time (Jo Kaasi tan taje kabira, rame kaun nihora). It is said when he died, many sects fought, to do his last rituals as per their believes, but when the cloth uncovered from his body, there were only flowers and nothing else.

The seat to lead the *Yagya* is empty and then next *Yogi*, i.e. Anger *Yogi* acquires the space, without wasting anytime, chanting of *Mantr* continued, like nothing happened. *Raavan* offered his first head to Lord *Shiv*.

Now Lord *Shiv* was also concerned, if *Raavan* really does so and kills himself, then *Ram's* motive to take this birth will be futile, establishing *Dharm* will not be possible.

But Lord will not come so easy, he will test *Raavan* till last moment.

9 months passed, all 9 *Raavan* brothers, dismantled themselves, no one is left except *Raavan*, *Ahiraavan*, *Meghnath* and *Kumbhkaran*. Now it was *Raavan's* turn, Ego head, had to offer to Lord *Shiv*, through *Agni dev* (Fire God).

Raavan was angry, he came on main seat and calls *Mahadev- Hey Mahadev*, I will sacrifice myself to you, if you do not come and give me final key to consecrate, subtle body.

Raavan sat on lead *Yogi* seat and brought his famous drum, started 1008 verses of *Shiv Tandav Strotam* in extempore. It was second time *Raavan* was trapped, he had no other way except, *Shiv Tandav Strotam*.

जटाटवीगलज्जलप्रवाहपावितस्थले
गलेऽवलम्ब्य लम्बितां भुजङ्गतुङ्गमालिकाम् ।
डमड्डमड्डमड्डमन्निनादवड्डमर्वयं
चकार चण्डताण्डवं तनोतु नः शिवः शिवम् ॥१॥

Jatatavigalajjala pravahapavitasthale
Galeavalambya lambitam bhujangatungamalikam |
Damad damad damaddama ninadavadamarvayam
Chakara chandtandavam tanotu nah shivah shivam ||*1*||

जटाकटाहसम्भ्रमभ्रमन्निलिम्पनिर्झरी_
विलोलवीचिवल्लरीविराजमानमूर्धनि ।
धगद्धगद्धगज्जलल्ललाटपट्टपावके
किशोरचन्द्रशेखरे रतिः प्रतिक्षणं मम ॥२॥

Jata kata hasambhrama bhramanilimpanirjhari
Vilolavichivalarai virajamanamurdhani |
Dhagadhagadhagajjva lalalata pattapavake
Kishora chandrashekhare ratih pratikshanam mama ||2||

धराधरेन्द्रनन्दिनीविलासबन्धुबन्धुर
स्फुरद्दिगन्तसन्ततिप्रमोदमानमानसे ।
कृपाकटाक्षधोरणीनिरुद्धदुर्धरापदि
क्वचिद्दिगम्बरे मनो विनोदमेतु वस्तुनि ॥३॥

Dharadharendrana ndinivilasabandhubandhura
Sphuradigantasantati pramodamanamanase |
Krupakatakshadhorani nirudhadurdharapadi
Kvachidigambare manovinodametuvastuni ||3||

जटाभुजङ्गपिङ्गलस्फुरत्फणामणिप्रभा
कदम्बकुङ्कुमद्रवप्रलिप्तदिग्वधूमुखे ।
मदान्धसिन्धुरस्फुरत्त्वगुत्तरीयमेदुरे
मनो विनोदमद्भुतं बिभर्तु भूतभर्तरि ॥४॥

Jata bhujan gapingala sphuratphanamaniprabha
Kadambakunkuma dravapralipta digvadhumukhe |
Madandha sindhu rasphuratvagutariyamedure
Mano vinodamadbhutam bibhartu bhutabhartari ||4||

सहस्रलोचनप्रभृत्यशेषलेखशेखर_
प्रसूनधूलिधोरणी विधूसराङ्घ्रिपीठभूः ।
भुजङ्गराजमालया निबद्धजाटजूटकः
श्रियै चिराय जायतां चकोरबन्धुशेखरः ॥५॥

Sahasra lochana prabhritya sheshalekhashekhara
Prasuna dhulidhorani vidhusaranghripithabhuh |
Bhujangaraja malaya nibaddhajatajutaka
Shriyai chiraya jayatam chakora bandhushekharah ||5||

ललाटचत्वरज्वलद्धनञ्जयस्फुलिङ्गभा_
निपीतपञ्चसायकं नमन्निलिम्पनायकम् ।
सुधामयूखलेखया विराजमानशेखरं
महाकपालिसम्पदेशिरोजटालमस्तु नः ॥६॥

Lalata chatvarajvaladhanajnjayasphulingabha
Nipitapajnchasayakam namannilimpanayakam |
Sudha mayukha lekhaya virajamanashekharam
Maha kapali sampade shirojatalamastu nah ||6||

करालभालपट्टिकाधगद्धगद्धगज्ज्वलद्_
धनञ्जयाहुतीकृतप्रचण्डपञ्चसायके ।
धराधरेन्द्रनन्दिनीकुचाग्रचित्रपत्रक
प्रकल्पनैकशिल्पिनि त्रिलोचने रतिर्मम ॥७॥

Karala bhala pattikadhagaddhagaddhagajjvala
Ddhanajnjaya hutikruta prachandapajnchasayake |
Dharadharendra nandini kuchagrachitrapatraka
Prakalpanaikashilpini trilochane ratirmama ||7||

नवीनमेघमण्डली निरुद्धदुर्धरस्फुरत्_
कुहूनिशीथिनीतमः प्रबन्धबद्धकन्धरः ।
निलिम्पनिर्झरीधरस्तनोतु कृत्तिसिन्धुरः
कलानिधानबन्धुरः श्रियं जगद्धुरंधरः ॥८॥

Navina megha mandali niruddhadurdharasphurat
Kuhu nishithinitamah prabandhabaddhakandharah |
Nilimpanirjhari dharastanotu krutti sindhurah
Kalanidhanabandhurah shriyam jagaddhurandharah ||8||

प्रफुल्लनीलपङ्कजप्रपञ्चकालिमप्रभा_
वलम्बिकण्ठकन्दलीरुचिप्रबद्धकन्धरम् ।
स्मरच्छिदं पुरच्छिदं भवच्छिदं मखच्छिदं
गजच्छिदान्धकच्छिदं तमन्तकच्छिदं भजे ॥९॥

Praphulla nila pankaja prapajnchakalimchatha
Vdambi kanthakandali raruchi prabaddhakandharam |
Smarachchidam purachchhidam bhavachchidam makhachchidam
Gajachchidandhakachidam tamamtakachchidam bhaje ||9||

अखर्वसर्वमङ्गलाकलाकदम्बमञ्जरी_
रसप्रवाहमाधुरीविजृम्भणामधुव्रतम् ।
स्मरान्तकं पुरान्तकं भवान्तकं मखान्तकं
गजान्तकान्धकान्तकं तमन्तकान्तकं भजे ॥१०॥

Akharvagarvasarvamangala kalakadambamajnjari
Rasapravaha madhuri vijrumbhana madhuvratam |
Smarantakam purantakam bhavantakam makhantakam
Gajantakandhakantakam tamantakantakam bhaje ||10||

जयत्वदभ्रविभ्रमभ्रमद्भुजङ्गमश्वसद्_
विनिर्गमत्क्रमस्फुरत्करालभालहव्यवाट् ।
धिमिद्धिमिद्धिमिध्वनन्मृदङ्गतुङ्गमङ्गल_
ध्वनिक्रमप्रवर्तितप्रचण्डताण्डवः शिवः ॥११॥

Jayatvadabhravibhrama bhramadbhujangamasafur
Dhigdhigdhi nirgamatkarala bhaal havyavat |
Dhimiddhimiddhimidhva nanmrudangatungamangala
Dhvanikramapravartita prachanda tandavah shivah ||*11*||

दृषद्विचित्रतल्पयोर्भुजङ्गमौक्तिकस्रजोर्
गरिष्ठरत्नलोष्ठयोः सुहृद्विपक्षपक्षयोः ।
तृणारविन्दचक्षुषोः प्रजामहीमहेन्द्रयोः
समप्रवृत्तिकः कदा सदाशिवं भजाम्यहम् ॥१२॥

Drushadvichitratalpayor bhujanga mauktikasrajor
Garishtharatnaloshthayoh suhrudvipakshapakshayoh |
Trushnaravindachakshushoh prajamahimahendrayoh
Sama pravartayanmanah kada sadashivam bhajamyaham
||*12*||

कदा निलिम्पनिर्झरीनिकुञ्जकोटरे वसन्
विमुक्तदुर्मतिः सदा शिरःस्थमञ्जलिं वहन् ।
विमुक्तलोललोचनो ललामभाललग्नकः
शिवेति मन्त्रमुच्चरन्कदा सुखी भवाम्यहम् ॥१३॥

Kada nilimpanirjhari nikujnjakotare vasanh
Vimuktadurmatih sada shirah sthamajnjalim vahanh |
Vimuktalolalochano lalamabhalalagnakah
Shiveti mantramuchcharan sada sukhi bhavamyaham ||*13*||

इमं हि नित्यमेवमुक्तमुत्तमोत्तमं स्तवं
पठन्स्मरन्ब्रुवन्नरो विशुद्धिमेतिसंततम् ।
हरे गुरौ सुभक्तिमाशु याति नान्यथा गतिं
विमोहनं हि देहिनां सुशङ्करस्य चिन्तनम् ॥१४॥

Imam hi nityameva muktamuttamottamam stavam
Pathansmaran bruvannaro vishuddhimeti santatam |
Hare gurau subhaktimashu yati nanyatha gatim
Vimohanam hi dehinam sushankarasya chintanam ||14||

पूजावसानसमये दशवक्त्रगीतं यः
शम्भुपूजनपरं पठति प्रदोषे ।
तस्य स्थिरां रथगजेन्द्रतुरङ्गयुक्तां
लक्ष्मीं सदैव सुमुखीं प्रददाति शम्भुः ॥१५॥

Puja vasanasamaye dashavaktragitam
Yah shambhupujanaparam pathati pradoshhe |
Tasya sthiram rathagajendraturangayuktam
Lakshmim sadaiva sumukhim pradadati shambhuh ||15||

Lord *Shiv's* doubt was clear, *Raavan* donated 9 heads, he will not stop, he will kill himself. *Mahadev* was lost in thoughts when *Tandav Strotam* touched him. Same heavy voice, extempore singing, one verse after another, over that *Raavan's Damroo* (Drum) beat.

Lord *Shiv* as always lost in the music played by *Raavan*, engrossed so much in the music, that tears started rolling from his eyes automatically. Each drop of tear turned into *Rudraksh* beads, and started spilling everywhere, he started dancing.

Shiv Tandav started, he was dancing so fast that no one could see Lord *Shiv*, only a beam of light in the sky was visible.

Men, Women, Deities, Demons, *Gandharv*, *Asur*, *Yaksh*, all mesmerised to see this miracle, *Gandharv* could not stop themselves to dance. The whole cosmos electrified with the energy, every creature felt the magic.

The light of Lord *Shiv* moved towards *Yagya Shala.* He was smiling, crying, and dancing. *Mahadev* was so mesmerized; No one in the *Yagya Shala* could see him because of intense speed at which *Mahadev* was dancing, but due to intense dance, a drop of his sweat dropped at the lotus flower.

As the drop of sweat from *Mahadev* touched the lotus flower, the dance of Lord *Shiv* stopped, and he was visible to *Raavan,* he stopped singing.

Mahadev said to *Raavan,* you forced me once again to help you, you offered 9 heads to me and your Egoistic head is also bowing down, I have to bless you, and give you key knowledge to consecrate a subtle body. But mind one thing, still you will not get *Sita.*

Raavan was obliged, he was still bowing down, he apologized and promised, he will never touch *Sita,* without her wish.

Adiyogi left, *Raavan* started the process of consecration of subtle body, how to form a figure and activate *Buddhi* in the energetic field and develop *Chitt* to store memories and *Karm.*

On the other hand, *Ram Setu* was ready, here Subtle body was ready.

On one side, Lord *Ram* completed impossible task by making a bridge on the Ocean, here *Raavan* completed impossible task by consecrating a subtle body, without any womb, without any *Sanchit Karm,* a subtle body, which was totally blank at karmic level, there was not even single memory or impression on its *Chitt* present.

A pure blissed form is generated in glass covered area, *Raavan, Ahiraavan, Meghnath* and *Kumbhakaran* can see the magic, how pure subtle figure is being created without a womb, no physical matter, no gross body, but still energetic, mindful, conscious and blissed form is appearing in a shape.

Just like Raavan, heavily built, amazing height, ego while smiling, a grey coloured translucent floating figure, combination of Mann, Chitt, Buddhi and Ahankar formed, standing tall 4 feet above the ground. Laughing unstoppable.

All seven energy Chakr (Muladhar, Swadishthan, Manipur, Anahat, Vishuddhi, Agney and Sahasrar) were clearly visible, with three Nadis – Ida, Pingla and Sushumna all in red color.

Although the Anahat Chakr or Chakr of love was small and weaker compared to other Chakr.

Ego was quite strong in the figure, since Adhira's Chitt was born out of Raavan's Chitt, the figure looked quite strong and heavily built like Raavan and earth element added by Kumbhkaran was visible in the figure, as he was floating in proud, every sight of the figure was full of proud.

Hairs tied upside as a pony. Red eyes emanating fire, strong muscles in arms and calves. A black cloth like Dhoti wrapped on groin area, with cross body black Angvastra on upper body.

Raavan bloated seeing this body, *Ahiraavan*, *Kumbhakaran* and *Meghnath* were also stunned, this was the biggest *Tantra* (Black Magic) of *Treta Yug*, which came into existence because of *Raavan*. He named this figure as **Adhira.**

We can call it pure organic Artificial Intelligence. But an A.I. of highest level, which required no hardware, only software at highest level of consciousness. An A.I. without hardware which can think, which can upgrade itself and above all no age limit.

Creating and maintaining Artificial Intelligence system in today's time, is a big task, but if you have money, you can achieve anything today, that's why AI is everywhere in the world, it looks good and useful today, but no one know its long term effects.

We can understand this Subtle body like a machine less A.I., but the danger is multi fold, because consecrating is challenge but maintenance, is effortless and maintenance not for 40-50 years, even for 1000 years or 10,000 years, no support is required.

Adhira folds hands while floating in air and pays tribute to *Raavan*, *Ahiraavan*, *Meghnath* and *Kumbhkaran*.

Bowing down to his creators, he was equally happy and blissful for his formation, and he was thankful to *Raavan*.

Adhira said- Lord, I am thankful for your work you have done, Initially I was suspect full, that whether I will be completed or not but when I saw, you invoked Lord *Shiv*, it was confirmed that the greatest of greatest scientist, great *Raavan* will be able to consecrate me.

Raavan was not able to control his excitement, after consecrating *Adhira*, he became immortal, he was not afraid of death now, he was bowing down to Lord *Shiv* again and again, he again promised, I will not touch *Sita* without her own wish.

Meghnath started roaring like thundering clouds. *Kumbhkaran* was in peace, though he was not able to control his excitement, *Ahiraavan* was equally excited, he contributed to greatest of greatest *Tantra* in the universe.

Raavan's energy, collectively of his son, brother *Kumbhkaran*, *Ahiraavan* and his 9 *Yogi* brothers will exist till eternity in the cosmos.

One guard comes inside, giving the news that, *Ram* has finalized the *Ram Setu*, they are setting their camps outside *Lanka*.

Raavan gave lead of war to *Meghnath* and said, I am not interested any more in war, I need to discuss a lot with *Adhira*, go and take charge of war and leave me here only.

On the out skirts of *Lanka* on the twelfth month, *Bhadrapada Maas*, *Shri Ram* reached *Lanka*. *Vanar Sena* under leadership of *Sugriv* setup their cantonment.

The news of *Adhira*, spread in three *Loks*, All *Devtas*, *Yaksh*, *Gandharv*, *Vanar* worried.

All went to *Mahadev*, they prayed *Mahadev*, *Brahma* and *Vishnu*, they wanted to discuss on this consecration.

Lord *Vishnu* took birth as Lord *Ram* to end *Raavan*, but now he will be eternal, now who will control him.

Ram, *Hanumaan Ji* and whole *Vanar Sena* also received this news, there was even serious discussion in Lord *Ram* camp, *Vibhishan Ji*, *Sugriv Ji*, *Hanuman Ji*, *Lakshman Ji*, *Jaamvant Ji* and many more were eager to know the consequences, and how future will look like, does it even matter now if *Raavan* is killed or not.

Sri Ram was quiet and peaceful, after listening all the questions, he started replying, this war is still important, nothing has changed, this war is initiated to establish *Dharm* and still much needed.

As of now *Raavan* is in physical form and because of him lot of *Rakshas*, are controlling different parts of earth and all three *Loks*. With this *Yudh*, *Raavan* will call his all leaders and Army generals from different part of the earth for this war.

We will be able to clean Mother earth from all such lethal *Rakshas* in one go, we need not to wander every corner of earth to search and kill them. So, this war is very much important to establish *Dharm*, again on the earth as it was earlier, nothing has changed.

Second about *Raavan's* eternity, *Adhira* is not *Raavan*, he is collective energy of *Raavan*, *Ahiraavan*, *Kumbhkaran*, *Meghnath* and *Raavan's* 9 brothers, which is not in physical form, He will exist for 1000s of years, but as of now, he will not be able to pick a grass flock even, for next few years, he still needs time to mature and improve, though he can be improved, but coming in full human form and controlling earth and three *Loks* like *Raavan* has done, is next to impossible, not in next 10,000 years nor even in next 100,000 years.

He can train, mentor and accommodate any human being, but he will not be able to become *Raavan*.

Adhira will be able to affect those, whose tendency is malefic, people with wrong intuition will be affected by him. Good souls will never be affected. Where negative energies are concentrated, where malefic people live and work, those who work in such environment will be affected.

Lord *Ram* continued, lets focus on fight, and continue our preparations, this is *Dharm Yudh* and we need to set example, that even most powerful person in all three *Loks*, if he abducts any women, they will not be spared.

Jaamvant asked, Lord, it may be the case that, in this period of *Treta Yug* there will be fewer evil spirits, but in the next *Yug* and beyond that, there will be more evil spirits in *Kaliyug*, so is it not so, that in future, *Raavan* will rule everywhere in *Kaliyug*?

Lord *Ram* smiled and said, *Jaamwant Ji* you are absolutely right, but as of now our duty is to establish *Dharm* in this period, so let's focus on present, anyway we have *Hanuman*, who is master of *Ashta Siddhi* (8 accomplishments) and *Nav Nidhi* (9 Treasures), who can overcome any such body. He will be able to deal with him.

'अष्ट सिद्धि नव निधि के दाता, असवर दीन्ह जानकी माता'

The above line comes from Hanuman Chalisa, written by Goswami Tulsidas Ji, it means that Ma Sita, blessed Hanuman Ji with 8 great traits, which are impossible for humans to attain, a person if tries, he or she can attain one or two traits, but getting all 8 in one lifetime is impossible. There is a Shlok on this as well:

अणिमा महिमा चैव लघिमा गरिमा तथा |
प्राप्तिः प्राकाम्यमीशित्वं वशित्वं चाष्ट सिद्धयः ||

This Shlok explains names of those 8 traits, that are as follows: Anima (Minimise body to size of atom), Mahima (Expand size at any length), Garima (To become infinitely heavy), Laghima (to become weightless), Prapti (The one who can get anything, He/she wishes), Prakamya (to reach core of earth, fly and stay in water for anytime), Ishitva (To become a deity) and Vashitva (to control anything). She also blessed him with 9 treasures or Nidhi. These 9 treasures belong to Lord Kuber only.

1. पद्म निधि (Padam Nidhi), 2. महापद्म निधि (Mahapadam Nidhi), 3. नील निधि (Neel Nidhi), 4. मुकुंद निधि (Mukund Nidhi), 5. नंद निधि (Nand Nidhi), 6. मकर निधि (Makar Nidhi), 7. कच्छप निधि (Kachhap Nidhi), 8. शंख निधि (Shankh Nidhi) and 9. खर्व (Kharva) or मिश्र निधि (Mishr Nidhi).

Jamwant Ji again asked, so Lord, are you giving responsibility of monitoring *Adhira*, to *Hanuman*?

Lord *Ram* said, I think there can be no better option than *Hanuman*.

Hanuman Ji was standing there, he happily promised to control *Adhira*.

Lord *Ram* continued, our *Trimurti* lords must have some plans in future to control *Adhira*, so don't worry about future, leave it to them only.

Everyone was quite satisfied, what *Prabhu Sri Ram* said, they understood that, war is necessary, and brining *Ma Sita* back should be our prime objective now, then, there was loud applause- *Jai Sri Ram, Jai Sri Ram, Jai Sri Ram, Jai Sri Ram.*

Vanar Sena was ready to conquest *Lanka* and bring *Mata Sita* to *Sri Ram*.

Before the war started, many proposals came to *Raavan* to return *Sita Ji* and end the war, *Angad*, *Hanuman Ji*, and then *Vibhishan* all came to convince *Raavan*, but *Raavan's* arrogance was at its peak, he did not want to settle down, nor he was distraught by the outcome of the battle.

Most of *Raavan's* time used to spent in the *Yagya shala*, like a child forgets everything when a new toy comes in his hand. *Raavan* also lost sense of time and situation.

The war started and every day, one by one *Raavan's* army started decreasing, many lethal and ferocious *Rakshas* were finished by Lord *Ram* and *Vanar Sena*.

Meghnath comes to rescue and injures *Lakshman* to level of coma. *Raavan* thought that *Meghnath* will be able to take care of everything, but he forgot, that *Meghnath* is in front of Lord *Vishnu* himself as Lord *Ram* and *Sheshnag* as *Lakshman Ji* and above that, they both are with their beloved *Hanuman Ji*, the master of 8 *Sidhis*.

Finally, *Hanuman Ji* brought whole *Dronagiri* mountain from *Himalaya* to *Lanka* and cured *Lakshman Ji* with *Sanjivani booti*, after that, *Meghnath* could not be spared from *Lakshman Ji*.

Kumbhakaran also went to the battlefield at the behest of *Raavan*, he also proved to be very disastrous to *Vanar Sena*, but at the end of the day, he also attained *Moksh* at the hands of Lord *Ram*, after *Kumbhkaran*, *Ahiraavan* also sacrificed to *Raavan's* ego.

After that, it looked like death became synonymous of *Lanka*. No warrior left in *Lanka*, no *Rakshas*, no Army General, was there to lead *Raavan* army. No Son, no brother left there.

एक लाख पूत सवा लाख नाती, ता रावण घर दिया न बाती

As told by Lord *Ram, Raavan* unleashed his greatest and most terrifying demons and *Tantrik* from all the three *Lok* into the battle. No one was spared, Mother Earth was happy, all the demons had been killed in the fire of war, Lord *Ram* hailed in all the three *Loks*.

When *Ahiraavan*, *Meghnath* and *Kumbhkaran* died, *Raavan* had to enter the battlefield. *Adhira* also requested to *Raavan* that, now you have to take the lead, else *Lanka* will be lost.

On the seventh day of war, *Raavan* came to battlefield, he proved to be disastrous as his name was, till evening no one could find any way to kill *Raavan*, then *Vibhishan* came and he told Lord *Ram* to shoot on his navel, which is his source of life.

When Lord *Ram* shot arrow in his navel, *Raavan* called *Adhira* to give him final instructions, how to be safe and improve himself and help his desires to be fulfilled by his progeny, he also instructed *Adhira* to help everyone, left from his progeny to keep safe and alive.

While *Raavan* was talking to *Adhira*, *Sri Ram* and *Hanuman Ji* could see this from distance, *Sri Ram* told *Lakshman Ji* to go near *Raavan* and check what he is doing with *Adhira*, *Lakshman Ji* was confused and terrified, I can't see *Adhira* and *Bhaiyya* and *Hanuman Ji* can see him easily, what's wrong with me.

Anyway, *Lakshman Ji* goes there and stand towards *Raavan's* head, *Raavan* immediately stopped the discussion, *Lakshman Ji* said- Hey *Raavan* I know you are talking to *Adhira*, but I am also here for last minute knowledge from you, you have proved world after consecrating *Adhira* that there is no one like you.

Can you give me some knowledge, which I can use to serve my bother when he will be at throne of *Ayodhya.*

Raavan was angry, *Lakshman* you came for knowledge, and you don't know how to stand in front of your *Guru.*

Laxman knew that if *Adhira* is there, he would be standing near *Raavan's* feet, and because of *Adhira, Lakshman Ji* stayed near his head, but *Raavan* denied, to talk, so *Lakshman Ji* went to *Raavan's* feet, he could feel some heat, he was sensing someone else is also here.

Raavan understood the purpose of *Lakshman Ji,* though he gave great knowledge to *Lakshman Ji* on *Raj Dharm* and *Dharm* of younger brother, *Dharm* to serve a king.

When *Lakshman Ji* left, *Raavan* told *Adhira* before leaving, that I will come back, time to time and give you instructions as what to do and how this world will be again under *Raavan's* reign.

As of now *Raavan* requested *Adhira,* to energise every left-out person in *Lanka* and give proper funeral to all dead *Rakshas.*

This took one year for *Adhira* to settle *Lanka* and help *Vibhishan* in the process, while *Vibhishan* also regrouped the whole clan, who were left out here and there, injured, absconders, widowers and orphans.

When Lord *Ram* returned to *Ayodhya* with *Lakshman Ji* and *Sita Ji* along with *Vanar Sena. Vibhishan* held the throne of *Lanka. Sri Ram* instructed *Hanuman Ji* to go back to *Lanka* and check what *Adhira* is doing and keep a tab on him.

Hanuman Ji used to travel *Lanka,* time to time and get updates by *Vibhishan* on *Adhira* and other issues and updated Lord *Ram* every time.

After some time *Hanumaan Ji's* frequency to visit *Lanka* elongated and *Lanka* was also settling down, there was no symbol of any kind of threat in *Lanka*, so all were relaxed, *Adhira* found this, as golden opportunity to initiate his master plan.

Later, *Adhira* trained and guided many strong descendants, born in *Raavan's* clan, who were able to handle *Raavan's* power and fulfill his wishes. They were trained and mentored by *Adhira*, to take *Lanka* back in their hands from *Vibhishan*, but *Hanumaan Ji* was there to handle the situation, So *Adhira* never succeeded.

This happened many times, So Lord *Ram* instructed *Hanumaan Ji* to control *Adhira* completely. After many failed trials, As per *Raavan's* suggestions, *Adhira* focused on southern part of *Aryavart*, since he also needed sometime to improve and upgrade himself.

Due to *Adhira's* work at start of *Dvapar Yug*, south of *Bharat* became *Dandak Aranyak* and *Lanka* disconnected with rest of *Bharat*. *Vibhishan* was focused on *Lanka* only, so the two lands *Bharat* and *Lanka* disconnected largely.

Rishi and people left that very large area of *Dandak Aranyak*, and *Adhira* controlled this land.

Years passed, situation in *Lanka* was under control.

In *Ayodhya*, *Ram Ji* served *Ayodhya's* throne, *Sita Ji* went to jungle again due to controversy in *Ayodhya* on *Sita Ji's* sanctity, *Luv* and *Kush* took birth, in *Rishi Valmiki's Ashram*. The time came when Lord *Ram* wanted to leave to his heavenly abode, *Luv* and *Kush* took the throne of *Ayodhya*, *Ram* and *Sita Ji* met again, but now they wanted to stay alone till eternity, so *Ram Ji* decided to leave along with other divine souls like *Bharat Ji, Shatrughan Ji, Lakshman Ji* and *Hanumaan Ji.*

But *Hanumaan Ji* decided not to leave, since *Sri Ram* himself ordered *Hanumaan Ji* to keep eye on *Adhira. Ram Ji* realised, unknowingly he gave *Hanumaan Ji* boon to be on earth till eternity.

Sri Ram left earth with *Lakshman Ji, Bharat Ji, Shatrughan Ji* and *Mata Sita.*

Hanumaan Ji stayed on Earth to keep eye on *Adhira.*

Jai Sri Ram

Discussion continued.........

Bhima stopped and picked a glass of water, when *Uma* interrupted, so you mean *Adhira* is behind cleansing our clan, but why? We are also Shaivaits, he is also Shaivait and formation of great *Shiv* Devotee *Raavan.*

Why on earth, a *Shiv* Devotee would like to kill another *Shiv* devotee.

Bhima replied, while keeping glass on the table- *Adhira* is behind all this but, that is not full story. As you remember Lord *Ram* mentioned, *Adhira* is a subtle form and cannot harm like a human being, but he can influence malefic souls, he can train and mentor.

Ajay suddenly exclaimed- So you mean he trained someone who is behind us.

Bhima chimed- yes exactly, *Adhira* is the mentor, and the enemy is someone else:

Achyutanand

Bhima again started narration.

CHAPTER 7

The Villain - Achyutanand

1995 AD, Kaliyug

In *Dandak Aranyak* (now a days limited to only dense jungles of South India), *Adhira* maintained *Raavan's* clan from *Treta Yug* to till date, this clan survived earth for 80,000 years with help of *Adhira*. In the deepest jungle of *Mangadu*, near *Rameshwaram* in *Tamil Nadu*, now there is another great *Shiv* devotee born in this clan.

Achyutanand from childhood had intense abhor for shallow *Shiv* Devotees, He could not stand, seeing everywhere *Shiv Ling, Jyotirlingas* and every second person, claims to be *Shiv* Devotee.

He used to question every such *Shiv* Devotee about *Adiyogi* and prove them by arguments and acts, that they are not real *Shiv* Devotee, with some arguments he used to prove shallowness in such *Shiv* devotees, as per him, this is not *Shiv* Devotion, what they are doing. Drinking alcohol, Smoking hashish, and just offer water and milk to *Shiv Ling* on every Monday is not *Shiv* Devotion. Real *Shiv* Devotion is to become *Shiv* himself, best in *Yog*, control tendencies like anger, greed, lust etc. A pure selfless nature, can only become a true *Shiv* Devotee.

Achyutanand was himself ardent devotee to *Adiyogi*, his compassion and knowledge to Lord *Shiv* was unmatchable, with same intensity he was follower of *Raavan*. He believed that no one could match the level of Devotion *Raavan* had for Lord *Shiv*. *Raavan* spoke extempore *Shiv Tandav Strotam*, a 1008 verses *Strot* which was created by *Raavan* instantaneously, so effective that *Shiv* engrossed in the *Strotam* when *Raavan* sang it, the *Strotam* was equal to Lord *Shiv's* frequency. Such level of love and devotion is unmatchable.

Achyutanand trained himself in childhood to sing *Shiv Tandav Strotam* in same intensity, as *Raavan* should have sang that time. *Adhira* was not fully consecrated, while *Raavan* last sang *Shiv Tandav Strotam*, so he was never able to complement, if *Achyutanand* has same frequency as *Raavan* or not.

Adhira started paying attention to *Achyutanand* from childhood and narrated many stories of *Raavan*.

Though being from *Raavan* clan, he was much better than *Raavan* in terms of lust and greed to materialistic life. But ego was equal to *Raavan*, he believed himself to be most eligible *Rakshas* till date after *Raavan*, who will reinstate *Raavan* reign again on earth.

This hate increased by age, against every *Shiv* Devotee on the earth who doesn't belong to *Raavan* clan. He hated, why so many *Shiv* temples consecrated in *India* and worldwide, and devotees never stop to surround Lord *Shiv*, any time in the day, they just want one or another wish to be full filled, by Lord *Shiv* and ready to reach every place where Lord *Shiv* tried to live, from *Rameswaram* to *Somnath* to *Amarnath*, *Kedarnath* and even *Kailash*.

This kind of Devotion by lakhs of people every time, disturbs great devotees like *Achyutanand* and *Raavan* to connect to Lord *Shiv*, He wanted complete attention of Lord *Shiv* on *Raavan* clan only, if Lord *Shiv* listens, then listen to *Raavan* sons only, if Lord *Shiv* gives any boon, then give only to *Raavan* sons, if Lord *Shiv* ever attends, then should attend to *Raavan* sons only.

Achyutanand disturbed more, when *Adhira* informed that, *Raavan* didn't got *Moksh* till date, even after getting death by Lord *Ram*, because Lord *Shiv* never forgave *Raavan*, for what he had done, he pleaded Lord *Shiv*, 1000 times but Lord *Shiv* denied.

Lord *Shiv* once said- I can forgive you *Raavan* for any misdeed you did, but when you abducted *Sita*, you came in form of a *Sadhu*, from that day onwards, people started disrespecting *Sadhus*, a perception created that a *Sadhu* standing on his or her door, may be a con like *Raavan*, not a real *Sadhu*. Real *Sadhus* don't get alms now. Any dacoit, fraudster abducts women and children having *Sadhu* attire, some steal in name of *Sadhus*, some are not *Sadhus* but they disguise and take alms and use in wrong ways, many have formed big temples and monasteries to earn money from public. For eternity you demeaned whole sect of *Sadhus* and for this, I cannot forgive you *Raavan*. Your punishment will set an example for those who, con like *Sadhus* to fulfill their desires, your punishment will remind every con *Sadhu* that they will not be forgiven by Lord *Shiv* himself.

Lord *Shiv* continued, even if I wish, your *Karm* will not set you free, because of such a heinous crime you did.

This was another reason *Achyutanand* wanted full devotion of Lord *Shiv* towards *Raavan* clan and may be in coming future, Lord *Shiv* forgive *Raavan* and he will attain *Moksh*.

He wanted exclusive rights of Lord *Shiv* to *Raavan* clan.

Adhira was waiting, for such a child in the lineage who could take place of *Raavan*, so *Adhira* trained him from childhood in every art including weaponry, *Yog*, martial arts, *Tantra Vidya*, Astrology and warfare including technical and biological warfare. He found *Achyutanand* capable to be real descendant of *Raavan*.

Under *Adhira's* mentorship by 2011, when *Achyutanand* was about 16 years of age, *Adhira* decided to test *Achyutanand* capabilities, first *Adhira* tested at level of knowledge, which *Achyutanand* passed very easily. *Achyutanand* had strong memory and he learned all *Ved, Puraan, Shruti*, etc by heart, especially text related to *Adiyogi*.

Then he was tested for his Yogic capabilities and there was no match of *Achyutanand* in *Kriya Yog*, *Hath Yog* and *Ashtang Yog*.

Then he was tested for battlefield and to surprise of *Adhira*, *Achyutanand* was quite ready to learn the skills.

It took only 2 years for *Achyutanand* to become a full trained fighter and warfare technologist. Now even a team of army soldiers could not stand him. *Adhira* gave him some secrets, which expanded *Achyutanand's* capabilities at mental, physical and internal level, beyond human capacities.

Now it was time for *Adhira* to give him real field experiences. *Adhira* asked *Achyutanand*, who he would like to fight, without any delay he said, I want to finish fake *Shiv* Devotees, this will be my tribute to Lord *Shiv* and my sacrificial offering to *Kul Pita Raavan*.

Adhira looked for some groups and then shortlisted some people, who are in the region.

There was a team of 4 *Sadhus*, who used to pray, smoke, drink near *Shiv Ling*, they all used to carry iron made *Trishul* (Trident) to show themselves as Lord *Shiv* devotee.

Adhira thought, such small group, will be safe to test *Achyutanand's* skills for the first time and gave first task to *Achyutanand*. Both agreed and planned to go on his bike at the secluded temple, in mid of the Jungle in *Mangadu* at mid night.

He went to the place as *Adhira* directed, *Adhira* was flowing in air and *Achyutanand* was following him on his bike like a live map guide, when he arrived, *Achyutanand* parked his bike, some 500 meters before the temple compound, so that the *Sadhus* don't run away or alerted with bike sound.

There was a *Shiv Ling* in the temple which merely had a roof and four pillars, it can be estimated that temple is no less than 100 years old. Outside the temple *Sadhus* burnt *Agni Kund* and were smoking Hashish, they were totally drunk, lying unconscious and continuously chanting *Bhole Bhole*. *Achyutanand* entered the compound silently.

As *Achyutanand* entered one *Sadhu* was asking to another one, hey *Kaalu* how much did you earned today. *Kaalu* replied, these people are very innocent, wherever I go, I don't have to do too much, I just utter *Bhole-Bhole* and everyone give me something, either eatable or money. This is best way to live life, *Kaalu* said while laughing.

Achyutanand was not able to hear all this non-sense, fooling people in name of Lord *Shiv*, he immediately jumped in front of them, *Sadhus* got shocked, their intoxication blew away in a moment.

Achyutanand fired on them, you are not *Sadhu*, you fool people in name of *Mahadev*, you don't deserve to live.

All *Sadhus* looked at *Achyutanand*, a young boy, heavily built, rage in eyes, black cargo pants and tight fit black T-Shirt with heavy black shoes, was standing in front of them.

All *Sadhus* laughed at *Achyutanand* and asked who you are young boy, hey young boy just leave this place, your parent would be worried for you, kids like you should not roam in jungle at mid night, suddenly one *Sadhu* took one more puff from his *Chillam* and teased *Achyutanand*, *Bholenath* has sent his young soldier to give us a lesson and he kept laughing.

One of them tried to bully *Achyutanand*, *Kaalu* poked Trident to *Adhira*, go kid, go to your home, this is not right place for you.

In next moment, *Kaalu* had no arm to hold Trident. He fainted and fell down, rest three got angry and attacked *Achyutanand* together, *Achyutanand* moved one step back and whirled his sword in circle, in next moment, all *Sadhus* were down. Three heads rolled towards the *Agni Kund*.

Adhira called *Achyutanand*, come child, lets go, we need to leave this place, but *Achyutanand* thought something, and he finished the fainted *Kaalu* as well, he didn't wanted to leave any witness for what happened here.

Adhira smiled and both ran towards *Achyutanand's* bike and left the place in a moment.

Adhira then increased the level of field trials, group of 4 to group of 10 and 50 and then complete villages.

But when it came to mass destruction, he trained him to use disguise for killings not direct attacks, he used many methods like 100 needle attack with unidentified poisons, like 'Ricin' which comes from Castor oil plants. DNA based attacks so that even in crowd of 10,000 people, only those few people will be attacked by poisonous gas, who has a particular set of DNA structure.

For direct attacks, he had *Raavan's Dashanan Chakr* and *Vimshathiti Chakr*, which were kept safe by *Adhira* till date. He equally had mastered today's ammunitions, he always believed that weapons of *Dvapara Yug* and *Treta yug* are more sophisticated, reliable and effective in attack, than today's weapons.

Adhira also molded *Vedic* weaponry as per todays requirements, so that, they can be easy to carry but more lethal than any other weapon, exists today.

In Treta Yug a Rakshas stole Lord Vishnu Ji's Sudarshan Chakr, when he was not able to hide it, he went to Raavan and handed over the Sudarshan Chakr to Raavan. Raavan made a copy and developed Dashanan Chakr (10 Chakr), and returned the original one to Lord Vishnu.

He made a platform disc (Chakr) which can accommodate 10 small sharp discs, magnetically charged on platform disc, so that they can come back and land on same platform, after attack.

Now when he projects Dashanan Chakr, 10 small Chakr launches from the main platform Chakr, the devastation multiplies 10 times, because now instead of 1 Chakr, 11 Chakras are projected to attack at one time.

Raavan further improved and upscaled Dashanan Chakr to Vimshathiti Chakr (20 Chakr) and further Panchaashat Chakr (50 Chakr).

Now *Achyutanand* was alone enough for a platoon. *Adhira's* next job was to make his small team of fighters and serve him like leader.

Adhira was mentoring such kids in many places in *Dandak Aranyak,* he selected 8 such strong boys of his age, to become his team member. *Kaali* was best out of all, he was a great fighter, as well trustworthy follower.

Achyutanand became the leader of the clan in a year and then he declared war against all *Shiv* Devotees, all those Shaivait, who are out of *Raavan's* clan or those who do not believe in *Raavan's* doctrine. On this event *Adhira* gifted *Raavan's Chandra-haas* sword to *Adhira*. Which used to appear to *Raavan* whenever he wanted.

At the age of 21, Achyutanand looks no less than a monster, long beard, tall 8 feet height, thick curly black hairs, various scars on face and body, his left arm from elbow was mutilated in a war, he used a mechanical iron limb with iron fingers with a hook and knife double swap. He used to wear black cargo pants, tight fit black t-shirt and heavy black shoes. Big wide belt with 10 headed buckle.

On his back, he wore a black and grey metallic shining thin armour strapped in cross at chest with a buckle in shape of Trident, The armour had many surprises for the opponents like – sword, shield, needle arrow bow and many more things, which appears only when Achyutanand invokes with use of different handles, buttons and levers on armour belt.

He used open Thar black jeep, they changed the tires in ultra wide size, which made this Thar Jeep even more deadlier vehicle.

Many great *Sadhus* were attacked in *Himalaya*, Because of which many great *Yogi* moved towards *Shambala* in Mount *Kailash*. Where *Achyutanand* could not reach, not even *Adhira*.

> *Shambhala, Hsi-Tien, Belovoyde or simply Shangri-La it has many names. Many texts in different religions mentions Shambala such as KaalChakr Tantra. Vishnu Purana mentions Shambala as birth place of Lord Vishnu incarnation Kalki. Many religions and sects have different opinion about its location, name and relevance. Most profound location is said to be below Kailash Mountain in Himalayas, where only great Yogi, Chiranjivis and Nirmankaya can enter.*

When there were only few *Sadhus* left in the *Himalayas*, *Adhira* wanted to divert *Achyutanand's* focus towards strong Shaivait clans, because *Adhira* experienced that these clans are main breeding ground for such great *Sadhus*, so *Adhira* told him to select some strong clans, where *Markandey* clan was the first to choose.

Achyutanand was trained enough in accidental killing, so most of his attacks looked like accidents or mysterious deaths.

His knowledge on poisons, hidden attacks, and small arms, like needles with poison which will detect as heart attack was impeccable. His knowledge on herbs and trees was also great, he can create his weapon out of anything.

Now he became, so fierce that he could kill 100s of people in blink of eye. His skills on traditional weapons like- Bow and Arrow, Spades, Swords etc., became too good. Today's best team of 20 warriors could not stand against him even for 2 mins.

That was the reason, he was able to do such mass murders in *Purali* and then *Kaithi*.

After Adhira's instructions, he focused only on *Markandey* clan, and started eliminating one by one, many great people were targeted, including one priest in *Bali* and then *Achyutanand* went to Switzerland to Kill *Mahesh* Sir, *Samikshit's* father, and likewise in span of 1 to 1.5 years, many such murders happened one by one. But since it was start, they did everything in suspenseful manner, they didn't wanted, Law and order agencies to be after them. To avoid attention, they spared *Kaithi* village till sometime back, because, this village was famous for *Markandey* clan, and as they would have done anything in *Kaithi* then, *Guru Aksi* would have somehow convinced Government that, there is someone who is against only *Markandey* people.

But since now, they were desperate, so they took such a big step, to attack on whole *Kaithi* village, because *Samikshit* was there and he will be 16 on next day of *Maha-Shivaratri*. As *Samikshit* will be 16, *Adhira* new that he will become invincible and *Achyutanand* could not kill him, how and where, they didn't knew, but this was confirmed, that *Guru Aksi* was only waiting for this day, that's why they took such a big step, that, no one should be spared in *Kaithi* and they again tried to hide the killing, which they even succeeded.

Adhira came to know about *Samikshit* only 1.5 years back, when *Achyutanand* was doing mass murders in *Himalaya*, that a soul in *Markandey* clan has taken birth, who will become reason to kill *Achyutanand*.

If anyone can save the *Markandey* clan then it is only *Samikshit*, so he first came to *Chennai*, they could not find you there, so he kept searching the whole country, they found that you came to *Kaithi* but only for few hours and then disappeared, after many months, they found that, you people are living in disguise in *Purali* and they reached *Purali*, where he destroyed the whole village, and when he came to know that *Samikshit* was saved even from there, he came to *Kaithi*. Someone was definitely, giving them information in your village.

Guru Aksi came to know about *Purali*, then we were told that all the people of *Kaithi* should come here to *Nandpuri*.

Discussion continued.........

While explaining, *Bhima* looked towards the *Markandeyi*, every one's eyes were wet. *Uma* was sobbing for a long time.

Ajay could not stop him and said cryingly, this means my father is no more, he has killed everyone in the village.

Uma could not control her anger, fear and helplessness. She screamed- Hey *Mahadev*, what have you done, this one man has killed my whole family, my whole clan for a stupid reason.

She screamed loudly- Why, why did you enabled *Raavan* to create such a lethal weapon.

All people in the village gathered near *Uma*, *Samikshit*, *Ajay*, *Rudr* and *Jogi*.

Bhima's wife, *Damayanti* came to solace *Uma*. *Bhima* hugged *Ajay*.

Everyone was crying in the village.

Bhima found it difficult to compose everyone, the situation was quite tensed and fearful.

Bhima came to *Ajay* and *Samikshit* and pacified both, my friend, I understand your pain, but what I have told till now was the negative part of the story, there is a solution given by *Mahadev* himself. We don't have too much time, if you all allow me then, let me finish what I was saying and let's join our forces, forces of Shaivaits and *Vaishnav*, to fight this evil force.

Some villagers brought water for everyone and calmed them, so that *Bhima* could finish what he was saying.

Samikshit was crying remembering his father, when he heard *Bhima*, he exclaimed, you said that, I would be the cause of his death, but how?

Bhima said, absolutely you are the savior of this clan and the reason for the death of *Achyutanand* but, not alone you need someone's company.

Now, I will tell you the secret which *Adhira* still don't know, that, how *Samikshit* will become invincible and how he will be reason to kill *Achyutanand*.

Bhima again drinks a glass of water and continues his story.

This intrigued everyone in the village, all glued to the ground to know the great secret.

CHAPTER 8

Adhira's Contrary

5500 Years BC, Dvapar Yuga

Krishna at his youth realised about *Adhira* because both *Ram* and *Krishna* are incarnation of Lord *Vishnu,* both has same *Chitt.*

Krishna saw how so many sinful souls have taken birth in *Dvapara Yug* because of *Adhira,* from *Putna* to *Kans, Jarasandh, Shakuni, Duryodhan, Duhshasan,* and so many *Rakshas,* Demons, Vampires and Witches.

Earth was full of sinners, infact the effect was so bad that, the war in *Treta Yug* which happened between two kings from two countries, *Ram* and *Raavan,* now has entered the families.

> *As per many Vedic scholars, In these 4 Yug cycle, each Yug is represented as a cow, having 4 legs of Dharma or Adharm. In Satyug, the cow was standing on 4 legs of Dharma, there was no Adharma, people were content, they were happy what they had, no body lies, no one had greed.*
>
> *In Treta, one leg became symbol of Adharma, and three legs, left of Dharm, that's why demons started breeding up, Raavan born in Treta Yug.*

In Dvapar (Dva means Two and Par is synonym to legs), Dharma and Adharm were equal, that's why the hatred cropped up so much, war and jealousy entered in families, In Treta Yug, we saw how Lakshman Ji, left his comfort, for service of his brother and sister-in-Law Sita Ji. Bharat Ji slept below ground, for 14 years because, his brother Ram will sleep on ground for next 14 years, while his own mother took this promise from Raja Dashrath only for benefit of Bharat, so that he can become king of Ayodhya, but Bharat even didn't touched the throne, on the other side, in Dvapar, we saw how Pandav and Kauravs were fighting for throne.

In Kaliyug, Adharm overtook Dharm, now only one leg of cow is left of Dharm and three legs became symbol of Adharm.

Krishna had to kill his *Mama Kans*. *Kauravs* and *Pandavs* were anti to each other. *Shishupal*, *Krishna's* cousine like *Pandavs* hated *Krishna* very much. Families and Royal families were under cold war internally for throne. King *Drupad* insulted his childhood friend *Guru Dron* for some piece of land, he even forgot his promise, he gave to *Dron* in childhood. *Krishna* could see a major war is on the verge.

Adhira was not able to take over *Lanka* but he somewhere disbalanced *Dharm* and *Adharm* to very high level, like it was in *Raavan's* reign.

The only difference was that, in that time all Demons and *Rakshas* were under *Raavan's* control, but now they were free and running their own nexus.

So, *Krishna* decided to counter the effect of *Adhira* and develop a divine subtle form, which will generate better human beings and counter balance *Adhira's* effect.

Krishna killed *Kansa*, his maternal uncle, freed his grandfather *Raja Ugrasen*, mother and father, *Devaki* and *Vasudev*. *Raja Ugrasen* once again held throne of *Mathura*.

Then *Krishna* started working on consecrating a divine subtle form, *Krishna* invited many *Yogi* and *Gurus* of that time to perform great *yagn*, to make a form, which can sustain millions of years in *Kaliyug* and uplift humans and generate better *Yogi* and *Sadhu* in *Kaliyug* and counterbalance *Adhira's* destructions.

Some *Yogi* told him that, once *Yogi Sunira* also tried to do so in this very *Yug*, *Dvapar Yug*, but he was not successful.

Krishna formed a team and searched for *Sunira* and entrusted that team, with the task of working on *Sunira*, but even after many years, they did not get success, then Lord *Krishna* went towards Mount *Kailash* to seek help from *Mahadev*.

Krishna was a genius, we see him as flute player and then lord who gave immense knowledge of Gita, but that was not his only identity in human form, he was a great lover and poet, he could hypnotise people with his flute, he was a great architect, who made an amazing palace in the sea. He was a great politician who caused great Mahabharat war to establish Dharm. He handled weapons like Sudarshan Chakr, which was not easy for any fighter of that time. He became great teacher after giving Gita sermons. He taught people of his village to worship mountains instead of Indra. He taught to love their cattle for own health benefits and improve economics.

He also improved many things coming from Treta Yug and even from earlier times, for example the Sudarshan Chakr. The Sudarshan Chakr which was improved by Raavan to Vimshathiti Chakr (20 Chakr) and further Paanchashat Chakr (50 Chakr).

Krishna further improved and made Shatam (100) Chakr and even Sahasr (1000) Chakr.

He even developed Vish Dhumika Chakr (A Chakr which emanates poisonous Cyanide gas to kill whole army instantly).

Krishna also developed anti-Chakr to be saved from attack of such Chakr, he called it Chakr-Haas. A disc which can call all Chakr sent by attacker on his platform parent disc, without causing any harm to his own Army.

Krishna was confident that he will be able to consecrate a subtle form.

Almost after 1 year of *Dhyan* and *Tap* in *Himalaya*, Lord *Shiv* came to see *Krishna*.

Krishna bowed down to Lord *Shiv* and Lord *Shiv* greeted *Krishna*. *Krishna* explained his reason for calling Lord *Shiv* from *Dhyan*. *Adhira* has disbalanced the earth again with *Dharm* and *Adharm*.

Mahadev is a Nirmankaya, he does not remain in physical form all the time, when required he appears in physical state or partial physical state, but for that it takes power of penance and meditation, and It takes time as well, not only the power of Mahadev but also power of the seeker, the higher the quality of the seeker, the sooner he can help Mahadev to come into the form of creation, with his or her own energies. That's why it is said that, God also needs a true devotee, God and the devotee are not different. Raavan had that power that he could call Mahadev, the same power was there in Krishna, so Mahadev appeared, but it is necessary to take time.

Adiyogi smiled and replied, you know better, there is reason behind everything. If *Adhira* would have not consecrated that time, then *Raavan* would have killed himself, and then *Ram's* birth would have gone in vain. Because the war happened that time, the earth was free of such demons, for so many thousand years, now the time has repeated, and I know you will find some solution.

Lord *Krishna* said, that he helped *Sunira* but he was not successful, so I want to create a divine subtle body which can counter balance *Adhira*, and can also generate good souls.

Adiyogi looked worried – he said that without my help, *Sunira* started doing such work after *Raavan* and he reached to a successful limit as well, if I give you this knowledge too, then there is possibility that in coming future, world may compete to create their own Subtle bodies. Everyone starts fulfilling their desires by creating a subtle body, these subtle bodies improve themselves, they cannot die, because they are not physical, their knowledge has no limit, they can wander anywhere in the universe. There is no restriction, if this happens then at one time maybe man will fight for their own existence only because of these subtle figures.

Imagine these forms as todays AI (Artificial Intelligence). What Adiyogi concerned 7500 years ago, today we are again in same situation and dilemma with AI. That time Adiyogi had control of subtle forms for consecration, but today there is no control, anybody can design and develop their own AI. Businessmen are behind AI to develop and improve day by day. There are many institutions in the world to look after and monitor, but still, AI is not centrally controlled and if it goes in wrong hands imagine what will be our future. May be Homo Sapien's future is left only for few more years and then only Machines will rule this planet.

An Artificial Intelligence enabled Robot, is probably mentioned as Rakshas Kali in many Vedic texts.

You know better what the consequences could be. If one *Adhira* can cause so much imbalance, imagine if such 10-15 subtle figures are consecrated, then what would happen.

Lord *Shiv* explained that *Hanumaan Ji* is there till eternity, who has *Asht Siddhi* to control such forms.

Krishna argued that *Hanumaan Ji* has done great job till date, because of him *Adhira* is still under control, but he is Lord *Ram* devotee, he even if desires, he cannot devote full time for a soul like *Adhira*, because as somewhere *Ram* name is hailed with full love and devotion, *Hanumaan Ji* will move to that place knowingly or unknowingly, he has already dedicated himself for Lord *Ram*, and no one else. We need to have a form which can give full time to look after *Adhira*.

The debate went on for many days, both of them gave their arguments, finally Lord *Shiv* agreed, but he took a promise from Lord *Krishna,* that you will remove this knowledge from your *Chitt,* this knowledge should not remain on earth in any form and as he said this, Lord *Shiv* disappeared.

Krishna agreed and came back to *Mathura* to start work on consecrating divine subtle forms. Many *Sadhus, Yogi* came to *Mathura,* for this great work, everyone wanted to add some value from their side to this great work.

It took *Krishna* almost 10 years of continuous *Yagya* and efforts to consecrate the subtle form. After 10 years of great work:

A pure white coloured air formed a human figure in padmasan, with four components Mann, Chitt, Buddhi and Ahankar and four energy Chakr were visible- Anahat, Vishuddhi, Ajna and Sahasara. Three Naadis, Sushumna, Ida and Pingla were clearly visible, all in bluish green color. Lower three Chakr were absent, which are symbol of food, shelter, lust, desires etc.

A small pony on head, smile on face, body covered with white clothes, lean body, long hands and fingers, belly little bit out showing constant Pranayam effect. Floating in Padmasan, four feet above the ground.

Krishna named him **Kaalyogi**.

Kaalyogi bowed down to Lord *Krishna,* and also bowed down to all the *Yogi* and *Sadhu* present there.

Krishna greeted *Kaalyogi* and thanked Lord *Shiv* to help him and thanked *Kaalyogi* to take a form.

After this, Lord *Krishna* spent some time with *Kaalyogi* to tell him everything, from the abduction of Mother *Sita* to the creation of *Adhira*. He also instructed *Kaalyogi* that your task is to keep an eye on *Adhira*, to stop his misdeeds and to generate good souls, wherever *Adharm* is increasing, inspire the divine souls to leave the desire for liberation and take birth again.

These subtle bodies are not created from someone else's subtle body or soul, so no *Karm* or memory is imprinted on their *Chitt*, their memory storage is totally clean, they are born out of nothingness and will merge into nothingness. The first thoughts and impressions which Lord *Krishna* will evoke, those will be the first impressions imbibed on his *Chitt*. This is what *Raavan* did to *Adhira,* so he was devoted to *Raavan*, and now *Kaalyogi* will be devoted only to Lord *Krishna.*

Lord *Krishna* asked him to stay with him for some time, as *Kaalyogi* needed time to upgrade himself and till then it was also necessary to avoid *Adhira* for any attack on *Kaalyogi*, which could be easily avoided by staying with Lord *Krishna.*

After some time *Kaalyogi* started becoming self-sufficient, Lord *Krishna* also got busy in family conflicts and started establishing the kingdom in the *Dwarka.*

Within a few years, as seen by Lord *Krishna,* the Great *Mahabharat* war took place, *Adhira* had so much influence on the *Kaurav* army that the *Kauravs* went on doing misdeeds and *Adharm* one after the other. *Duryodhan* was the most affected, once he was so much influenced by *Adhira*, that he tried to arrest Lord *Krishna* himself, when Lord *Krishn* came to *Duryodhan* for dispute settlement, but then world knows, what happened to *Duryodhan.*

Duryodhan ko samjhane ko, Bhishan vidhwans bachane ko
Bhagwan Hastinapur aaye, Pandav ka sandesa laaye
Do nyay agar to aadha do, Par ismein bhi yadi badha ho
To de do kewal paanch graam, Rakho apni dharti tamaam
Hum wahi khushi se khayenge, Parijan par asi na uthayenge
Duryodhan wah bhi de na saka, Aashish samaj ki le na saka
Ulte Hari ko bandhne chala, Jo tha asadhy saadhne chala
Jab naash manuj par chhaata hai, Pehle vivek mar jata hai
Hari ne bhishan hunkar kiya, Apna swaroop vistaar kiya
Dag-mag dag-mag diggaj dole, Bhagwan kupit hokar bole
Zanjeer badha kar saadh mujhe, Han han Duryodhan bandh mujhe
Ye dekh gagan mujh mein lay hai, Ye dekh pawan mujhmein lay hai
Mujhmein vileen jhankar sakal, Mujhmein lay hai sansaar sakal

(*Bhima* was Lord *Krishn* devotee, he could not resist, while saying so and recited one section from third section of poem *Rashmirathi* by great Indian poet *Ramdhari Singh Dinkar*).

Adhira had so much influence on *Kauravs*, that even a great warrior like *Ashwathama* could not spare himself from *Adhira's* effect by the end of the war. At last he also turned into a demon in the end of the war, he cut off the heads of the five innocent children of *Draupadi* and then fired *Brahmastra* on *Uttara's* womb, the daughter-in-law of *Arjun*, to kill an unborn child, just to avoid *Pandavs* lineage to further develop.

By the end of the war, the earth became empty of human beings. Here two more *Chiranjeevi* came out from *Mahabharat, Kripacharya* and cursed *Chiranjeevi Ashwathama*.

Lord *Krishna* suffered a lot due to *Ashwathama's* misdeeds, he knew, this all happened because of *Adhira*. Here *Kaalyogi* was not fully prepared yet, he needed more time and *Kaliyug* was knocking at the door.

Then Lord *Krishna* played such a trick that no one could even imagine, even *Adhira* has not realised till date, but one day he will feel the pain, that how his own misdeeds, backfired him.

A few years after the war, even Lord *Krishna* left the earth, but before that he explained *Kaalyogi*, what would be his main responsibility in *Kaliyug*.

Kaalyogi inspired many great, *Yogi* and divine souls to take birth even before the beginning of *Kaliyug*, so that a good society could be established.

After the Great *Mahabharat* war, crores of souls were wandering, *Adhira* needed evil souls and *Kaalyogi* needed divine souls.

Some divine souls do not want to be trapped in the cycle of birth and death, they want to get out of this cycle of birth and death, some call it liberation, some Nirvan or Moksha. On the other hand, some divine souls do not want to take birth, because they find more pleasure in the subtle form, rather than living in the bondage of this world in the physical gross body. Kaalyogi ensured that he would persuade such divine souls to take birth at the right place, so that it would help in the establishment of Dharm.

Who will take birth from which womb or mother is not based on any one condition or any fixed formula, souls take birth in a womb, on the basis of their desires, acquired from the accumulated impression of their previous many births, which we call as Sanchit Karm.

It is not necessary that, a divine soul will take birth from divine parents only, we have seen many such examples like, Raavan was born to a Rakshasi mother and a sage father. A devotee like Prahlad became, son of a demon like Hiranyakashipu. Duryodhana was born in the Pandu clan. Kansa's father King Ugrasena and his sister Devaki were all divine souls, still he was born in such family. Such variations are seen everywhere, at all times. There is no basis for having religious children in a religious family and parents.

Let us understand this with an example, a play is going to start in an open amphi-theater, there is no ticket, no seat reservation, within few minutes the theater will be full of people, everyone will sit on some or the other seat, whether it is front, middle or last seat, corner or center, people are not forced to sit on any particular seat, rather they choose the place according to their unconscious mind's decision or we call it our Vasana, tendencies or Chitt's unconscious potential.

Similarly, souls take seat in a womb as per their Vasanas or tendencies.

Kaalyogi created such possibilities that great souls take birth and take birth at the right place and at the right time. We have seen many great reformers like *Adi Guru Shankaracharya*, *Meerabai*, *Chaitanya Mahaprabhu*, *Soordas*, *Goswami*

Tulsidas, Raskhan, Kabirdas, Mahavir Jain, Gautam Buddha, Karl Marx, *Swami Ramkrishn Paramhans, Chankya, Dalai Lama, Gurudev Rabindra Nath Tagore, Raja Ram Mohan Rai, Bhagwan Birsa Munda, Swami Vivekananda,* Nelson Mandela, taking birth on earth, when they were most needed.

You will get tired of taking names, but the list will never end.

With the advent of *Kaliyug,* evil spirits increased, but divine souls also did not lag behind, this world has given birth to many or in other words, in the history of human civilization, the most virtuous souls have taken birth in this *Kaliyug* of this *Manvantar.*

Pick any country, any religion, any field like Politics, religion, arts, wherever we would start counting, the names of divine souls will keep adding on. This is believed to be highest contribution of divine beings like *Kaalyogi* and may be such other divine beings as well.

Discussion continued..........

Bhima while saying, picked another glass of water.

Be it *Kaalyogi* or any other divine being, but we can definitely say that, we are the luckiest people to have been born in this *Yug* of such great souls.

Bhima looked at everyone once and this time, the scene was different, everyone had a wave of happiness running on their faces, all stood motionless with folded hands, listening to *Bhima.*

Samikshit's excitement was clearly visible, he came closer to *Bhima* and asked, where is *Kaalyogi*, is he around, can we meet him?

Bhima knew, everyone would be very curious, everyone would have many questions, but he first turned towards

Uma and said, so first I answer, the circumference of the *Ram* name we did yesternight.

Adhira is born out of *Raavan's Chitt*, his sub-conscious mind, unconscious mind, his feelings all are copied from *Raavan*, and hence his hatred and fear towards Lord *Ram* is also at same wavelength. See nature's magic he even can't come near the *Ram* name. That's why we inscribed *Ram* name everywhere, because of *Ram* name he will come near this village, but he will not be able to enter the village. He would be wandering here and there and must have called *Achyutanand* to come here, but he would not have single idea, what's going on here. But after few hours, he will also realise, how *Samikshit* will become invincible and how he will kill *Achyutanand*.

So, until *Achyutanand* reaches here with his army, we have time to prepare.

This time *Ajay* kept his hand on *Bhima's* shoulder and asked, friend, how do you know all this?

Bhima folded his hands and said, because I have also taken birth in this village only on the orders of *Sadguru Kaalyogi*, so that I can be useful at the right time.

Bhima continued, As *Adhira* was constructing his army, *Kaalyogi* was also preparing his army of divine souls.

Uma folded her hands and thanked *Kaalyogi*, she understood now, that the divine soul in *Purali* was none other than *Kaalyogi*.

Bhima also confirmed *Uma's* suspicion that *Maa Uma* had seen *Sadguru Kaalyogi* in *Purali*.

Everyone folded hands and silently bowed down to *Kaalyogi*.

CHAPTER 9

The War

Achyutanand's Contrary

Bhima continues- So now you understand who is our enemy, today he is focused on *Markandey* clan, but tomorrow he will attack another clan, that's why it's not only *Markandey* clan's responsibility, we all have to be together, to kill such demons and establish peace in the society.

There are always some evil spirits in every time, behind such malefic deeds.

Uma was still feeling uneasy, many questions were echoing. The biggest thought stinging her, that her son's name was coming again and again, that he is the savior, but he is an ordinary child, how on the earth, he will be able to face off with a warrior like *Achyutanand.*

A team of soldiers cannot handle him, who can move the mountains, where does my son stands against his capabilities, *Uma* was worried that her only son might also get killed in all this mayhem.

Bhima could clearly see *Uma's* pale face and her worries.

Before anyone could say anything, *Bhima* started saying, we do not have much time, now it's time to invoke *Kaalyogi*, he will be able to guide us for further course of action.

Bhima comes out of his verandah and walks towards the temple, people also follows him, in the open courtyard of the temple, he washes his hands and feet, sits on ground and starts chanting –

Bhima starts *Kaalyogi Ahvahan Mantr* –
ॐ अग्नये स्वाहा। इदं अग्नये इदं न मम॥
ॐ वां वायवे प्रारणधिपतये हरिण वाहनायांकुश हस्ताय सपरिवाराय नमः
ॐ जल बिम्बाय विद्महे निल पुरुषाये धीमही तन्नो वरूणः प्रचोदयात
ॐ आकाशाय च विद्महे नभो देवाय धीमहि, तन्नो गगनं प्रचोदयात्
ॐ पृथ्वीदेव्यै विद्महे सहस्रमूर्तयै धीमहि तन्नो पृथ्वीः प्रचोदयात्
ॐ *Kaalyogi* आवाह्यामि । ॐ *Kaalyogi* आसनं समर्पयामि॥

Cool breeze starts blowing in the temple area, thin fog covers whole area, as the mist clears, *Kaalyogi* is visible.

Kaalyogi appears, a very clear image of a Yogi, floating 4 feets above the ground, smiling face, very young and lean Ajanbahu[7] *body, covered with loin cloth, no ornaments, nothing on the body except the loin cloth.*

As he appeared, suddenly the atmosphere changed, his presence activated positive energy in every living being nearby. Every animal nearby started hoarding the place, where *Kaalyogi* appeared.

Everybody bows down to *Kaalyogi*. *Uma* and *Samikshit* were shocked for the first time to see a subtle body, visible so clear.

Kaalyogi smilingly said – *Aum Namah Shivay.*

---

[7] A person having long hands till knees, these are traits of divine souls, even Lord *Rama* was *Ajanbaju*.

I bow down to *Ma Uma*, the last descendent of *Markandey* clan, I bow down to *Ma Uma*, who gave birth to savior of *Markandey* clan, *Samikshit.*

Everybody stands with folded hands, circling *Kaalyogi* and looking him intensely.

It was no less than a miracle for everyone including *Bhima* who called *Kaalyogi.*

Bhima bow down to *Kaalyogi* and does *Dandvat Pranaam*[8].

Hey *Kaalyogi*, as per your instruction *Samikshit* is here, now please explain the next course of action for us.

Uma comes in front, she identifies him in first glance, with folded hands she asked, *Bhima* is saying that *Samikshit* will kill *Achyutanand*, is it true, are you also planning to use my son in this war, *Guru Ji.*

As *Uma* called *Kaalyogi*, *Guru*, knowingly or unknowingly what *Guru Aksi* said, proved to be real, *Markandeyi*, got their new *Guru.*

Ajay looked at *Uma* and tears rolled out on his cheeks, he remembered what his father said to everybody, two days back, he will be your *Guru. Ajay* was crying, he again murmured, he knew everything.

Kaalyogi smilingly looks everywhere and then looks towards *Uma* and says hey *Maa,* your son is blessed son, in his previous birth, he was great *Yogi* and before that he was a fierce warrior in *Maratha Sena* and like that for many births, his *Sanchit Karm* and *Chitt* is full of *Vedic* knowledge, *Yog*, Martial Arts and many great skills, to be an eligible fighter,

---

[8] Lying down dorsal on ground with stretched hands touching nose on earth

though your son is not going directly into the battle, so don't worry.

In this birth, he has already attained qualities of a *Yogi* and hence his body, mind and energies all are enough capable, to do for what he is born in this life. Because of his past life's qualities, many forces like me, supported him to take birth in this clan, from your womb, a great *Shiv* devotee and powerful women like you.

Everyone listening calmly to *Kaalyogi*.

Kaalyogi said, addressing *Uma* - As you know *Achyutanand* had finished *Markandey* clan and now he is after *Samikshit* and you, to finally finish the last descendant of this clan, but this is not his final goal, he will continue doing this with every ardent *Shiv* devotee and Shaivait clan, so it's time to stop him and kill him. Maybe after sometime, he moves towards innocent people or any other sect, god knows when he will stop, so it's not only *Markandey* clan's responsibility to stop him, it is our collective duty to stop *Achyutanand* and *Adhira*. That's why there is one warrior, who is going to help us, whom not one *Achyutanand,* infact 100 *Achyutanand* together could not face.

Our gods, always make plans 1000 of years ahead, we have a great warrior on this earth, very close to us, who will help us to stop *Achyutanand,* A great incarnation of Lord *Shiv*.

Uma looks at *Samikshit* and holds his hand tightly, her eyes were still wet.

Kaalyogi looks at *Uma* and understands her dilemma, so he removed the veil from this mystery.

To do so Lord *Krishna* already arranged a great warrior for us, his name is *Chiranjeevi Ashwathama*.

Ashwathama, Ashwathama, Ashwathama...... everybody murmurs this name.

Kaalyogi continues, you all know, how *Ashwathama* was cursed, but as you know, our lords do everything with some future plans.

On the night of the eighteenth day of the Great *Mahabharat* war, when *Ashwathama* and the *Kaurav* army were under effect of *Adhira*, *Ashwathama* did which was unimaginable.

After projecting *Brahmastra* on *Uttara's* womb, Lord *Krishna* could have killed *Ashwathama,* then and there. But he knew, *Ashwathama* is not the only culprit in this heinous crime, *Adhira* was equally part of it, so Lord *Krishna* planned to punish *Adhira*, with his own weapon, and cursed *Ashwathama* to be on earth as cursed *Chiranjeevi*.

Today, this cursed *Chiranjeevi,* who has been wandering in these forests for years, will help us and will also be free from the curse of Lord Shri *Krishna* and will also give befitting reply to *Adhira* for his deeds.

Lord *Krishna* entrusted me with the responsibility to help *Ashwathama* and that's why, I established this village, this village serves *Ashwathama*.

I trained *Ashwathama* to become *Nirmankaya*, to leave his cursed diseased body and stay in subtle form, because the way he was bleeding and diseased, he was not able to sustain 10 years. Sustaining 7000 years with such body was out of question.

It took him some years, to learn, how to live in subtle form and how to be *Nirmankaya*, then I taught him, how to take *Brahmastra* back after calling it, along with that, I trained him with many other weapons like *Sahasra Chakr,* invented by Lord *Krishna.*

Ashwathama got *Shatam* (100) *Chakr* and even *Sahasra* (1000) *Chakr* from Lord *Krishna* along with many other weapons.

He also got *Vish Dhumika Chakr*[9].

Ashwathama also learnt how, to be saved from *Sudarshan Chakr* attacks using *Chakr-Haas,* he learnt how to receive a *Sudarshan Chakr,* attacked by enemy on his own finger using his own platform *Chakr* disc.

After training him, I left him in this jungle and instructed to stay near any *Shiv* temple, he will be called in right time.

This village helps *Ashwathama* in many ways. Hundreds of temples near this village have been served by people of this village from ages.

As of now *Bhima* is head of this village and ready to serve *Ashwathama* as and when required.

Now it's time to call *Ashwathama.*

Kaalyogi continued, since he is a *Nirmankaya,* he cannot fight like a real human to faceoff *Achyutanand,* we need strong *Yogi* physical body like *Samikshit,* who can help *Ashwathama* to use his body for some time. He will adopt *Samikshit's* body, because only *Samikshit* has capacity to handle powers and energies of *Ashwathama.*

> *Every gross physical body has a limit, just like every machine has a limit on how much electricity it can run, how many thoughts and how much information it can*

---

[9] A *Chakr* which circulates poisonous gas cyanide to kill anyone instantly.

store, after how long time, it will start heating up, while running. Similarly, everybody, also has a limit, everybody cannot handle every soul.

The energy of a powerful soul can only be received by a powerful body, a body that is excellent in Yoga, that has conquered its senses, that has awakened its Chakr, and that has channeled the energy, flowing through its channels to its extreme limits.

Just like, when high voltage current comes in a light electric wire, the wire starts melting. Like when 500 watts of electricity enters a 100-watt bulb, that bulb explodes and shatters. A lesser capable body can not host a powerfull soul.

There is a mention in Ramayana, before the war and arrival of Lord Ram in Kishkindha. Baali challenged Hanuman Ji for fight, when Hanuman Ji was leaving for battlefield, Lord Brahma came and requested Hanuman Ji to take only 10% of his energies and rest transfer to his lord, before facing Baali. Hanuman Ji agreed.

As per Brahma Ji's boon when Baali came to fighting ground, Hanuman Ji's energies started transferring to Baali, initially he felt good, but soon he became nervous, he started sweating, he felt like whole cosmos energy is entering in his body, his nerves overloaded with energy and ready to burst, Lord Brahma came and told him to run away, else he will burst in 1000 pieces.

When Baali came to senses, Brahma Ji told Baali that, I requested Hanuman to carry only 10% of his energies, imagine what happened if he would have come with 100% energy.

Baali was not able to handle 5% of Hanuman Ji's energy, though he was the person, who defeated Raavan alone. To take the power of Hanuman Ji, the receiver had to be just like Hanuman Ji, similarly to absorb powers of Ashwathama, another Ashwathama is needed, even if his energy is dormant at present, but capacity is very much needed, which is only in Samikshit and no one else.

Kaalyogi continued, this is *Samikshit's* war, he is born for this objective, so *Samikshit* must go in the jungle and find out *Ashwathama,* he must be nearby, not too far.

After the arrival of *Ashwathama*, we will start further process.

Uma panicked and asked what is the procedure, *Guruvar*?

Kaalyogi continues…

As you all know, two souls cannot reside in one body, so *Samikshit* has to leave his body and *Ashwathama* will enter his body.

Mother's affection was coming in the middle of this work. *Uma* feared badly, she started crying, what are you saying *Kaalyogi*, my son, he cannot do such transformations, he is just a child. He doesn't know anything yet. I am very scared, lest I lose my only son.

Kaalyogi calmly says, don't worry *Uma*, I will always be there with *Samikshit*, try to understand, *Samikshit* is the only person who is capable of handling energy of *Ashwathama,* since he was a fighter and *Yogi* in his past many lives, his *Sanchit Karm* is warehouse of martials arts and *Kriya Yog* and spirituality from many past lives, and *Ashwathama* is great fighter, incarnation of Lord *Shiv*. *Samikshit* is born for a purpose and he has to do his duty in this birth, as a Shaivait, you must understand it very well.

You know that *Ashwathama* is the *Rudr* incarnation of Lord *Shiv*, he will get place only in the body, blessed by Lord *Shiv*.

100 of fighters like *Achyutanand* cannot sustain the force, knowledge and experience of *Ashwathama*, but without a pious, Yogic and strong body, *Ashwathama* cannot do this. Destiny has chosen your son for this task.

Adhira must be on our borders and *Achyutanand* can reach any time with his army.

We don't have time and there is lot to do, if this experiment is not done in time, then we all will be destroyed like *Purali* and *Kaithi*.

Uma understands and agrees with heavy heart and eyes full of tears. She looks at *Samikshit*, kisses his forehead and leaves to worship Lord *Shiv* in the temple.

She requests last time; can someone accompany him when he goes to find *Ashwathama. Kaalyogi* didn't liked the idea, but it was matter of *Samikshit's* safety, so he orders *Bhima* and *Ajay* to accompany him.

Kaalyogi suggests them to stay near temples, *Ashwathama* is more likely to be found near *Shiv* temples.

Bhima brings his jeep, *Samikshit* and *Ajay* hopped on and enter the forest and started looking for the temples.

Kaalyogi instructed *Bhima* to carry some tools like spade, digging bar, pick axe etc.

While *Samikshit* locates *Ashwathama*, *Kaalyogi* will make the rest of the preparations in the village, he calls *Rudr* and *Jogi*.

Ajay opened his phone, while Jeep enters the jungle, but there was no signal in the phone, to see the map, so he asked *Bhima* if he has physical map of this area, since it's his territory, *Bhima* replied don't worry, I know all temples here and I have met *Ashwathama* many times in these temples, so we will try first from those temples in the way, which I know.

Bhima moved towards *Asirgarh* fort direction, towards south-east from their village *Nandpuri*.

They kept going deep inside the jungle, but they had no idea how to find a subtle body. *Samikshit* was tensed, He can't be seen, he can't be heard, he can't be touched, so how I am supposed to find him. *Bhima* said, when I need to meet *Kaalyogi,* I chant *Ahavahan mantr* for *Kaalyogi*, he is also *Nirmankaya,* maybe you can try some *Ahavahan mantr.*

Samikshit didn't agreed, I don't think so, neither I know, what kind of *Mantr* will be used to call *Ashwathama,* let me meditate, maybe I get some solution.

Bhima stopped the Jeep near some plateau rocks, all three deboarded and *Samikshit* moved towards a higher plain rock, he sat down and started for meditation, he was quite tensed, he prayed to Lord *Shiv* before meditation and requested, if he is really a good devotee, help him to accumulate all his energies in meditation and trace *Ashwathama.*

As he closed his eyes, *Ajay* and *Bhima* both were jaw dropped.

As *Samikshit* closed his eyes in meditation, he started raising above the ground and this time, *Samikshit* kept raising and raising and raising. *Samikshit* rose above the jungle's normal tree's height. Slowly slowly all disturbances gone, *Samikshit* went into trance, he couldn't hear anything. *Ajay* and *Bhima* screamed once, when they saw *Samikshit* raising so high, but he couldn't hear anything, complete silence and then he hears *Shambhu Shambhu* in very low sound, barely audible to normal persons, *Ajay* and *Bhima* couldn't hear, but because of *Samikshit* incredible Yogic practices he can hear sounds below 6 decibels, as the voice hits his ears, he started coming to senses and he started landing back to his place slowly. He opened his eyes and saw *Bhima* and *Ajay* both were staring at him, with jaw dropped stare.

Samikshit enquired what happened, why are you looking so strangely, *Bhima* replied, strangely? man you were flying like a helicopter in the air, I have never seen anyone meditating so deeply, your *Udan Vayu*[10] is greatly active. I have never seen any physical gross body, raising above the ground so high in my life.

Ajay nodded, yes, we heard about *Samikshit* and I saw him sometimes in his childhood, but it was merely some centimeters above the ground, this time you literally crossed the jungle height, how is it possible?

Samikshit couldn't understand, since he was also not aware, well I felt the air differently every moment in meditation, silence increased each moment, but I was not sure that, I was raising so high.

---

[10] Our body has 5 type or air or *panch vayu,* which are used for different purposes, *Praan Vayu, Udaan Vayu, Samana Vayu, Apana Vayu* and *Vyan Vayu. Udan Vayu* helps for buoyancy in our body, which helps us to float, jump, run while not feeling our actual body weight.

Anyway, leave this and let's move to right side, I heard some voices in very low decibels.

All came back to the jeep and moved fast, towards the direction, *Samikshit* pointed towards a temple, they halted and started walking towards the temple.

Bhima exclaimed, yes, I know this temple, it's *Gupteshwar Mahadev* Temple, *Ashwathama* comes here regularly.

Samikshit started walking towards the temple and looked everywhere, but he could not find any person, the sounds were coming exactly near *Shiv Ling*, like someone is sitting there and chanting *Shambhu… Shambhu..*

He folded his hands and politely asked in direction of the sound – "Who is this blessed soul, here chanting"

Unknown man- *Shambhu Shambhu…..*

Unknown man- …… अतीव अभाग्यम् वयस्कः अस्मि

Samikshit- अहो भाग्यम् देवर्षि, you speak Sanskrit, do you belong to our community since, I have not seen anyone else outside our Markandey clan, who speaks Sanskrit and why can't I see you.

Unknown man- *Markandey* clan?

Suddenly the unknown man's voice becomes strong, a fine glimpse of figure is visible.

A strong figure, 6.5 feet height, heavily built body, dusky complexion, long hairs, strong aura, fiery eyes, like Lord Shiv himself sitting in padmasan.

Unknown man-I don't belong to any clan, but you are definitely, *Samikshit.*

Samikshit replies, ok so you are *Guru Drona's* son *Ashwathama.*

Samikshit bows with folded hands and says, yes, I am *Samikshit,* one of the few survivors of the *Markandey* clan.

Ashwathama looks at *Bhima* and *Ajay,* he knows *Bhima,* smiled at him, *Bhima* also bowed down with folded hands.

Ajay still couldn't believe his eyes, he saw two, bodiless figures in a single day, one of whom, was the one, everyone had been hearing about, since their childhood, the Great *Ashwathama.* So many stories, fake incidences and appearance have been reported on him from centuries, don't know if *Ashwathama* ever appeared to anyone or not, but today he was there, clearly visible, not to a single person, infact 3 persons at one time.

There are very few lucky people in this world, who get to see a *Chiranjeevi,* today *Ajay* was also one of those lucky ones.

Chiranjeevi and Immortals these are two different words and two different states, A Chiranjeevi is not immortal, they have set time limit and set objectives, they have been ordained with specific tasks, for example, Lord Parshuram is Chiranjeevi till Lord Kalki doesn't takes birth, once Lord Kalki is born and he gets all knowledge on weaponry from Lord Parshuram, he will leave this earth. Lord Parshuram has been ordained to train Kalki as his last disciple, to fight with demon Kali.

Ajay greeted with folded hands and introduced himself.

Ashwathama also politely accepted the greetings and consoled *Ajay* for the death of *Guru Aksi.*

Bhima met *Ashwathama* after many years, he always mesmerises, when he see such a strong *Nirmankaya* existing for last 7500 years, *Bhima* was compassionate towards *Ashwathama,* he feels the pain, *Ashwathama* was suffering for last 7500 years and today he was happy, he wanted to say a lot of things, he wanted to inform *Ashwathama,* that *Gurudev,* today you will repay your bad *Karm* and you will resurface as a great fighter and saviour of *Dharm.* The curse is going to end today, and *Ashwathama* will be called as great *Chiranjeevi* from today onwards instead of cursed *Chiranjeevi.*

Bhima was excited, *Ashwathama* saw *Bhima's* expression and he understood his excitement and smiled at him. But both could not say a single word.

Time was short, according to *Bhima's* spies, it had been several hours since *Achyutanand* and his army had left *Mangadu.*

That's why *Bhima* came straight to the point and said, *Guruvar* time has come, *Sadguru Kaalyogi* is waiting for you in *Nandpuri*.

Ashwathama laughed and said, so the day has come, when I will be free from my sins.

Samikshit understood the matter, yet he asked to hear it from *Ashwathama* himself (Literally from horse's mouth), I did not understand?

Ashwathama took a deep breath and said, I am cursed by Lord *Krishna,* because I tried to end *Pandav* clan, now, that merciful *Krishna* gave me opportunity, to neutralise my negative *Karm* by giving me opportunity to save *Markandey* clan.

Samikshit smiles, so let's go to *Sadguru Kaalyogi* and save me, my clan and this world from *Achyutanand.*

Ashwathama smiles and snaps, I am gone.

Bhima, *Ajay* and *Samikshit,* all astonished, what happened, has he already gone.

Samikshit screams, *Guruvar* don't leave us alone, you can travel in air but we can't, please wait for us.

Ashwathama comes back, hmm so we must go together, I guess this is what *Sadguru Kaalyogi's* plan, from now onwards we are one, so how can I leave you alone my son.

Ashwathama takes front seat of the Jeep, *Bhima* was on driving seat, *Samikshit* and *Ajay* sits on the back seat and Jeep moved towards, *Nandpuri* village.

After few minutes of drive, *Ashwathama* said that before going to war, I need my weapons, so take me towards *Asirgarh* fort.

Samikshit did not understand anything, so *Ashwathama* explained while jeep was moving toward *Asirgarh* fort.

It is one of the most oldest fort, around 700 years old, built by *Raja Asa Ahir*, before that there was a small cave here, where I kept my all weapons and I used to worship Lord *Shiv* here, along with Lord *Krishna,* but when King started building the fort, the labour tried to demolish the cave, I was furious, I started scaring them in ghostly ways, this play went on for many days, many true and fake *Tantrik* came to finish me, a great *Tantrik* came, he was *Aghori* and he recognized me, I told him the reason, then he ordered, that this cave could not be broken and at the behest of the king, this cave was closed from all sides and taken inside the fort.

I moved to other temples and left this one, I didn't needed weapons anyway, just wanted to offer, water to my *Mahadev*, so came here after a few hundred years and made a short cut to enter.

Ashwathama smiles, beings like us use such places to hide our important things, keep it reserved for our usage, else this world wants to evade every place, specially these archeologists, they dig up everything, everyplace, to trace history, so we have to make such ghostly arrangement in such places, to keep our things safely. Sometimes I wonder, you people have generated so many archeologists, big laboratories and waste so much of time and money and still don't get the right result, why don't they contact us directly and then *Ashwathama* laughs out loudly.

They reached inside the fort, *Samikshit* said while walking, and you know people are afraid to come to such a place that, it is haunted by some ghost or spirit, and then story after story piles up and the place becomes haunted forever.

Ashwathama laughed and said, it is good for beings like us, due to this fear, beings like us get a place to live peacefully.

They were standing in front of a wall in the lowest part of the fort.

Ashwathama says ok now let's not waste time, break the wall and enter into the cave. All brought some tools to break the wall, from the Jeep, which helped them to break it.

It took around 15 minutes to make a way, they could see a cave entrance which was covered totally with spider webs.

When they cleared the webs, a cave was visible, they all entered the cave, it was quite long and big, they all walked inside the cave, following *Ashwathama,* at very end of one corner, there was a big amber resin in square shape standing tall in front of *Samikshit.*

A big wall of Amber resin in light orange mixed red color, though the cave was very deep in the fort, sunrays were coming there, which were passing through the amber resin, creating a shining rock feel of Amber.

Ashwathama's weapons were opaquely visible from the resin wall, A bow, and two spears, they can see easily.

Ashwathama directs *Samikshit* to pick a bottle of liquid, kept in one shelf made in wall, looks like bare hands made it, just to keep the bottle, he instructs him to pour whole liquid on the amber.

In five minutes, the amber is gone and all weapons fell on the cart.

Samikshit was amazed to see such great weapons from Mahabharat times. Bow, arrows, sword, Mace, spears, *Shatam Sudarshan Chakr* and *Sahsara Sudarshan Chakr*.

All were shining like just came from factory after polish, each weapon was quite heavy, *Samikshit* used his full power to lift the bow, he was barely able to handle the bow with his full power. *Ashwathama* smiled, hey young boy, you are not able to handle my bow with both hands, while I used to carry it, all the time during war.

Samikshit pantingly said, *Guruvar,* I am a boy of *Kaliyug,* and I am not military trained, I never fought any fight, it's too much for me. *Ajay* and *Bhima* helped *Samikshit* to put all the weapons in the cart.

Ashwathama and all laughed on *Samikshit's* innocence, while leaving the cave, *Samikshit* drove the weapon cart somehow pouring all his muscle power, *Bhima* and *Ajay* helped him.

It took them around 30 mins, to come out of the cave and fort, where their Jeep was standing, they boarded all the weapons on the Jeep and left the cart there only.

Samikshit asked, what should we do with this cart?

Ashwathama smiled and said, leave it here, may be some Archeologists find some value in this many 1000 years old cart. It belongs to my time.

On the way *Samikshit* told to *Ashwathama,* what happened to him. Ashwathama said, that Kaalyogi told him all these incidences and told me that, time is coming to end my curse and end of this demon *Achyutanand*, from that time, I am waiting in these temples.

Ashwathama narrated his story, he started from his childhood, when his father, went to meet King *Drupad* and he denied to help us, then father came to *Hastinapur* and started teaching *Kauravs*. To the last day of *Mahabharat* war, when *Adhira* influenced him completely and then how he met *Kaalyogi* and then how he learnt taking *Brahmastra* back from *Kaalyogi* and then many more things.

Today, probably these three people must have heard, the real story of *Mahabharat* without any mixup.

Bhima's eyes welled up with tears after listening to *Ashwathama*. Hardly anyone had heard the *Mahabharat* from *Ashwathama's* perspective, till date, this was a different story, the story of *Ashwathama,* who was so pious, since childhood that he did not even liked his father's discrimination with the rest of his disciples, but by the last day of the war, nobody knew how on earth he became a demon.

Samikshit said, now you have told everything in brief, one day I will sit down and will listen complete *Mahabharat* story from you in detail.

Ashwathama laughed and said, of course son lets finish *Achyutanand* today, then maybe we will get, lot of time, when we can talk and share.

Ajay said, *Guruvar* is this kindness limited to *Samikshit* only?

Ashwathama assured, no friend, everyone who wants to listen is invited.

6 hours passed in the whole journey, when they left *Nandpuri* village and back to the village, here everyone was waiting eagerly for them.

Here *Sadguru Kaalyogi* had got all the preparations done.

Ashwathama got down, everyone was waiting for him, as soon as he got down, *Bhima's* wife *Damayanti* brought a plate of *Aarti*, everyone honored him and touched his feet for blessings.

Today the whole village was seeing *Ashwathama* face to face for the first time, otherwise these people had only heard about him for thousands of years, only a few were lucky enough, to get to see *Ashwathama.*

The crowd of the village wanted to meet him, someone told that, I used to come to that temple, keeping *Belpatra* for you, some told that, I used to clean, that *Shiv* temple and some other *Shiv* temple.

Everyone described their own service, *Ashwathama* was happy to be part of it, it was a different day today, a lot was happening, it was a historic day for everyone.

Ashwathama was going to be freed from his curse today, the villagers saw two divine souls together for the first time. The *Markandeyis* were about to get their savior today.

After meeting everyone, *Ashwathama* went to *Kaalyogi* and bowed down to him, *Kaalyogi* is *Guru* of *Ashwathama* for the last 7500 years, *Kaalyogi* also blessed him – *Mukt Bhava*:.

A man came running to *Bhima* and said, 3 black jeeps have entered *Khandwa* border, they will be here in an hour.

Kaalyogi said, no, we should not allow them to enter the village.

Bhima ordered his army, until this process is completed, keep them away from the border of the village, May Lord *Hari Vishnu* keep you safe.

Bhima sent his army, but there was a fear in his mind, whether his army would be able to face those demons or not?

Here *Kaalyogi* asked *Ashwathama* and *Samikshit* to come to the temple, instructed *Samikshit* to wash his hands and face and take the seat.

Everyone was kept out, there were only four people inside the temple, *Kaalyogi*, *Ashwathama*, *Bhima* and *Samikshit*, the rest were standing outside the temple.

Both *Samikshit* and *Ashwathama* were seated face to face, a fire pit was lit in the middle and a large earthen pot containing water from the holy *Narmada* river.

Kaalyogi explained the process to both.

- *First of all Samikshit will go into Ardh (partial) Samadhi, by ejecting from his Sahasrar Chakr, and I will receive his Sukshm Sharir and Soul.*
- *Ashwathama will enter, into Samikshit's body through Sahasrar Chakr.*
- *Since this will be first transaction, Samikshit will not be able to handle the powers of Ashwathama, so he may fell down or vomit and not able to stand for some time, the reactions are unpredictable, just stay strong and quiet.*
- *Ashwathama also needs to be quiet, your powers will effect Samikshit's body, he would require time to handle your powers.*

Samikshit already exhausted his energies, while searching *Ashwathama*, so it is easy for him to meditate and perform the process easily[11], to accommodate *Ashwathama's* energies. Anyway, he already did this many times.

He traveled world in astral form, many times, nobody knew about it, but *Kaalyogi* knew this, so he was quite confident that, *Samikshit* will be able to handle the whole process.

When a person is strong physically and mentally, it is difficult by external forces to affect him or her. Either it is any emotion like fear, sadness or any negative energy or external forces like black magic, Tantra or wandering Souls.
It is only possible, when a person is weak mentally or physically, or not reached a certain level of maturity, like children below 18 years of age, or pregnant women or women having menstrual periods.
That is why, women, specially during pregnancy or menstruation and children below age of 18 are not suggested to go in some temples, which are specialised for Tantra Sadhna such as Shani temples, crematorium or graveyards like places.
A Child till age of 18 is not very stable mentally, he has lot of excitement, on the other hand, a pregnant woman or during menstruation, woman is week from inside, they can get under effect of such things easily.

---

[11] *Yogic Gurus* always suggest to do, some physical exercises before meditation, exhausted body can easily sit in meditation, because energy is consumed, which hinders to sit in one place.

Samikshit is very strong mentally, though he is below 18 years, but still till he don't allow himself and is feeling weak from inside, external forces cannot enter him.
As of now he was tired and he wanted that Ashwathama takes over his body, such transformation requires that your Ojas, allow such transformation without any resistance.

Kaalyogi asked both to go into meditation, the fire of the *Agni Kund* was lit. *Kaalyogi* was hovering around both of them, and *Bhima* was watching everything with folded hands.

Kaalyogi was constantly reciting *Mantr*, within a short while, there was a stir in the water pot, sometimes the fire in the fire pit was intense and sometimes it was very low, as if a small lamp was burning.

Within no time *Ashwathama* was gone, only *Samikshit* was there, *Samikshit's* body bathed in sweat, his body was changing, his shirt was tightening on his body.

After 10 minutes, the energy of *Samikshit's* body appeared in the form of a *Pinda* in hands of *Kaalyogi*, on the other hand, *Samikshit* fell down, completely wet in his own sweat.

Bhima tried to come near him, but *Kaalyogi* signaled him to stay away.

Samikshit turned towards earth and snored like a horse like, one wakes up after long unconscious sleep, when hit by some strong attack in fight, *Samikshit* started standing, pushing upwards with hands and knees, and sat in *Vajrasan* and huffed, *ufff* after such a long time, I can feel a body.

Kaalyogi smiled yes son, exactly after 7355 years, you can feel, how it feels to live in a body, infact in a healthy body without any scars, disease and ulcers.

Bhima was surprised, *Samikshit's* voice had changed.

He got up and bowed down to *Mahadev*, remembered *Shri Krishna* and *Vishnu Ji* and then bowed down to *Kaalyogi*.

Bhima's happiness was uncontrollable, he shouted out loud, **Hare Krishna, Hare Krishna, Hare Krishna**...... experiment successful.

Samikshit stands up, now he was not looking like slender boy, his height increased a little bit to 6.5 Feets, his arms stretched like a body builder, when he stood properly and raised arms towards sky, he was looking exactly like a *Mahayodha*, muscles in calves, arms shaped well, thick nerves were visible on his body, his *Shikha* was open and now long hairs added more grace on his personality, he was looking just like *Ashwathama* as people saw few minutes back. His voice also changed. He used to wear simple trouser and shirt, though the shirt teared out because of changes in his body, he was in his pants only, on the upper body, he was left with his *Janeu*[12] only.

Someone called *Uma*, she had been sitting in the temple since morning without taking food and water, as soon as she heard the news, she came running, seeing *Samikshit*, but when she saw, she could not understand who he is. My

---

[12] A sacred thread, *Pandits* give at age of 5 to 8 years to every child in the family, know as *Yagnopavit* ceremony, 3 cotton thread on left shoulder, represent obligation towards God, Parents and Teachers.

son *Samikshit* or *Ashwathama*? Should I hug him or bow down?

Samikshit folded hands and sat at *Uma's* feet, and said mother don't worry, I am your son, either you see me as *Samikshit* or as *Ashwathama,* I will remain your son.

Uma lovingly caressed his head and hugged him.

Meanwhile, three boys came running and shouted, they have come, three Jeeps are parked outside our village perimeter, one of them is a mad man talking something in the air.

Ashwathama wasted no time and lifted the bow from the Jeep, other weapons and equipment, seeing this *Ajay* and *Bhima* laughed. *Ashwathama* understood and said, don't laugh, now I am not that *Samikshit* anymore, it is the power of *Guru Ashwathama,* that I am able to lift this bow so easily, then he strung the bow, tied the quiver on his back, sword on left hand side waist, two spears also stuck on his back and went barefoot towards the forest. He told everyone to stay here, he could handle alone now.

But *Kaalyogi*, *Ajay*, *Bhima* and some soldiers kept following him.

At a distance of about 1-2 kms, there was some movement, *Ashwathama* prepared for the war, rest stood at safer distance.

Ashwathama Faceoff with Achyutanand

On the outskirt of village, due to *Ram* name written everywhere, *Adhira* was not able to enter the village, while he was here, since last night. When he was sure that everyone is here, he informed *Achyutanand.*

On the other side, *Achyutanand* also came with his entire contingent this time, *Kaali* had failed to kill *Samikshit* in *Kaithi* and on the other hand, he survived even after demolishing such a huge mountain in *Purali*, so this time *Achyutanand* came with full preparation.

But he was unware, what has happened here since last night, due to *Ram* name.

Adhira stopped outside, he asked *Achyutanand* and his troop to go inside, *Achyutanand* and his teams greets, *Adhira*, *Adhira* blessed them for victory.

It was late afternoon, but the sun was still shining brightly.

Achyutanand, *Kaali* and eight soldiers were moving into the forest, when an arrow came whizzing by and pierced the cloth on the right shoulder of the soldier who was walking in last row, the bow penetrated in the tree, along with the soldier, the soldier hanged on the tree because of his dress.

Everyone was surprised to see, no one could have done this, except a vicious warrior, they thought that there would be no hindrance, but they realized that, these people have made some preparations this time.

Meanwhile *Samikshit* comes out, there was strong sunlight coming from behind, his face is not clearly visible, but it was visible to everyone that a warrior is standing, tall and broad, bow in hand, spear and arrows behind, Sword hanging on waist.

He was standing only 200 meters away, but even from such a distance, *Achyutanand* could feel his power and gruesomeness. A warrior, that too not from today's time, but of the *Vedic* era, *Markandeyi* must have brought some great help.

Achyutanand enquired who are you and why are blocking our path.

Ashwathama smiles and says, how does it matter to you, you wanted to kill this physical body, so this physical body is *Samikshit* for you, your prime enemy at this time.

Achyutanand is confused, you can't be *Samikshit*, I have never seen him, but I know he is not a fighter like you.

Ashwathama laughed, so you are afraid to fight with warriors, you can kill only children and innocents, this is what your *Guru Adhira* has taught you.

Kaali was surprised, he knows everything about our *Guru* and us and he is not an easy warrior, *Achyutanand* was already fuming with anger, he ordered without listening to *Kaali*, attack him, let's see what kind of warrior he is.

Achyutanand could not tolerate the insult, he attacked *Ashwathama* by throwing a spear, *Ashwathama* bent slightly to one side and caught the spear while passing and threw it back at his soldier, who was hanging on tree, which directly crossed his chest.

Before *Kaali* could attack, *Ashwathama's* bow was raised once again, seven arrows came together and wounded the wrists of all seven soldiers, swords fell from all seven soldier's hands, the pain was so severe, that no one could hold the sword, all grounded due to severe pain.

Kaali was surprised, *Sapt Baan Vidya*, who is this man, who is so superior in archery.

Achyutanand said it would be fun, after a long time, he would face a great archer.

Ashwathama laughed, great archer, hmm in my time there was someone else who was great archer for my father.

Both were again confused, what he is saying, my time, my father.

Achyutanand now without thinking anything, signaled *Kaali* to attack with needles.

Kaali understood and pushed a button on his armor, A small bow, an arrow and a small thick cylinder comes out, he attaches the cylinder on hand rest of the bow and shoots the arrow on back of the cylinder, suddenly the cylinder burst out and many small needles fly towards *Ashwathama.*

Ashwathama knew about this weapon, when he saw the cylinder, he already took out his '*Shatam Sudarshan Chakr*' and the moment cylinder is busted, hundreds of small *Chakr* were revolving in the air, in form of shield, attached with each other, every tooth of every small *Chakr,* snapped to other *Chakr,* forming a larger shield and left no space, even air cannot pass through them.

All the needles collided with the *Chakr* and fell down, the *Chakr* came back to *Ashwathama,* after this *Ashwathama* did not lose even a single moment and started firing many arrows, one after the other on the enemies, the rain of arrows was such that no one was able to balance, somehow, *Kaali* and *Achyutanand* could save themselves, but rest 7 soldiers could not survive the rain, all were badly injured, the arrows were so strong that out of seven, only four survived, the remaining three were not able to move even.

Achyutanand understood, they can't overpower *Samikshit* in Bow and Arrow fight, he addressed all his soldiers- *Sons of Raavan, the enemy is in front, today is the time to die or kill, if you retreat, how will you face your Kulpita Raavan, he may be powerful, attack him together, kill him or sacrifice yourself. Raavan's sons cannot bow down.*

All soldiers fumed with energy, they tied their hands with a cloth, used their all power to lift the sword and ran towards *Ashwathama* in lightning speed.

Few steps before *Ashwathama*, one soldier who was at number two screamed to the first soldier, stop, he understood and ducked and second soldier came running and took a push on ducked soldier's back and attacked *Ashwathama* in the air, He wanted to cut *Ashwathama* in two pieces.

Ashwathama had already taken out the sword and shield, he started laughing while seeing this feat, as soon as the other soldier attacked with the sword jumping in the air, *Ashwathama* took the attack on his shield on his left hand, he did not move even a step, attacking soldier's sword broke in many pieces, soldier had no idea, that the shield would be made of 7000 years old metal, which weights almost 20 KGs.

As the sword broke, soldier lost his balance in air, *Ashwathama* slides his sword in his stomach, he was hanging in air, hooked on *Ashwathama's* sword.

Fear was clearly visible in everyone's eyes, here *Ashwathama* was again in same fire as he was 7500 years back, when he attacked, *Pandav* camp on the last night of the Great *Mahabharat* war. He chopped rest 3 soldiers one by one and moved towards *Kaali* and *Achyutanand*, While seeing *Kaali* and *Achyutanand, Samikshit* in the body was also not able to control himself.

He wanted to revenge his father, his father's uncle *Mahesh*, *Guru Aksi*, all *Markandeyis*, people of *Purali* and *Kaithi*, he wanted to revenge for all his loss.

Ashwathama rushed towards *Kaali* covered in blood and wanted to chop him too, *Achyutanand* understood, he felt that *Kaali* would not be able to handle it, he jumped in the middle and kicked *Ashwathama* hard, to divert *Ashwathama* towards him.

Achyutanand kick had power, *Ashwathama* realised, he is also no less powerful.

Ashwathama, moved towards *Achyutanand* and started attacking him with sword one after the other, without stopping, as if someone had started a sword machine, no automatic gun could shoot bullets as fast as *Ashwathama's* sword was attacking, *Achyutanand's* shield broke, his sword also broke into many pieces, he took another shields and swords fell nearby, but none could face the wrath. *Achyutanand* understood, if this continued for next 20 seconds, he will be divided into 100 pieces, so he jumped back, left his Sword, and called *Ashwathama* for a dual.

Ashwathama was not in mood of dual, he wanted to finish everything, but something inside called him, don't leave *Dharm*, if he dropped his weapons, then don't attack, last time when you left *Dharm*, you faced 7500 years of curse.

On hearing this, his anger calmed down, he stopped for a while and dropped his sword, *Achyutanand* felt it was the right time, he kicked *Ashwathama* hard on the leg, he staggered and fell down, *Achyutanand* held his leg and tried to throw him on the trees, but he failed, in the meantime, *Ashwathama* kicked *Achyutanand* hard on the chest, he rolled back many steps, *Ashwathama,* without losing time, caught *Achyutanand's* hand, lifted him up and threw away.

Before *Achyutanand* could wake up, *Ashwathama* jumped on his chest and started punching him, with his strong fist, one by one non-stop, *Achyutanand* was about to faint, his face swelled up, he could not even open his eyes, somehow, he kicked *Ashwathama* and saved himself.

He was not even able to face him in dual, his clothes were torn out, blood was oozing everywhere, he could hardly stand.

Kaali feared it, he thought something and threw a powder bomb, the whole area covered in dark cloud, *Ashwathama* could not see anything for few seconds, a dust storm rolled before him, in that moment *Kaali* holds *Achyutanand* and takes him back, that was no ordinary dust that was DNA coded dust, which didn't affect *Achyutanand* and *Kaali.*

Kaali said let's leave this place, *Guru Adhira,* must know about him, we will see him again, this is not right time, you are totally swelled and injured.

Achyutanand roared, no I am *Raavan's* son, I will not run away, I won't show my back.

Achyutanand was not ready to leave the battlefield, his eyes filled with blood, he wanted to retaliate, but *Kaali* pleaded, *Guru Adhira* is waiting outside let's go, we will come back and will see who this fighter is, but please leave now.

When *Achyutanand* didn't agreed, *Kaali* folded hands and apologized, I am sorry my Lord, I have to take you back, this is *Guru Adhira's* order to me.

Kaali blew something from his mouth and *Achyutanand* fell on *Kaali's* strong arms, *Kaali* took him on his shoulders and ran away.

Where they had their vehicles, he came out of the boundary and met *Adhira*.

Adhira when saw, he ordered to blow the area with fire, the fire was so fierce that no one could cross it. Everything started burning there, leaving no trace what happened here.

7500 Years Old Misdeed Backfired Adhira

On the other side *Bhima* and other villagers came to the site, as per *Kaalyogi* instructions. They all first blew off the fire with water and sand and then saw *Ashwathama,* he was standing strong and tall, but he too had lot of injuries and scratches, blood was coming from some parts of the body.

They brought a stretcher, but *Ashwathama* didn't want to go on stretcher, he walked back with the villagers. When he met *Kaalyogi*, he bowed down and thanked him, for all his support, today because of him only, *Samikshit* and *Markandey* clan is safe, because of him *Ashwathama* got a new life, because of him, he was able to finally come out of curse, he had on his soul for last 7500 years, of killing an unborn child and finishing a clan. Today *Ashwathama* saved a clan, his curse neutralised, his *Adharm* neutralised.

Kaalyogi in return thanks to Lord *Shiv* and *Krishna,* they are behind all this miracle, I am just a messenger and follower of Lord *Shiv* and *Krishna.*

Ashwathama hears a voice in his ears, Lord *Krishna* calls him, congratulations *Ashwathama,* finally you are free from my curse, now no one will call you cursed *Chiranjeevi,* you were a great fighter and a great son, and you will be remembered like that till eternity.

Ashwathama could not control himself, hearing these words, he wanted to leave, Sadguru *Kaalyogi* helped both of them, he turned the energy Pinda, towards *Ashwathama,* closed his eyes and *Samikshit* fell down, he was taken on a stretcher to the village hospital, *Uma* was there, *Samikshit* was getting bandaged, *Uma* was crying.

Villager were happy, they were cheering up we won, we won.

Uma was crying to see her son in wounds, but she was happy to know what happened, she is happier, that now they faced their enemy and enemy is gone, finally her son became the saviour.

She thanked *Kaalyogi* for believing in her son.

Kaalyogi said, the danger is not finished, *Achyutanand* is alive and so *Adhira*.

They will come back, and they will be back with more force, more power, more ammunition and well prepared.

Bhima said, *Gurudev* you are right but at least this time they know that, the fight will not be easy, it will not be a cakewalk for them that they come, finish the whole village and go back smilingly, like they did in *Purali* and *Kaithi*. This time their leader was nearly dead.

Kaalyogi smiled, yes you are right; but they also know this fact, they will prepare themselves, but next time we will attack them first.

Our experiment is successful, and we were able to do the transmigration in right time.

Everyone was happy, a good feast was prepared, it was time to thank *Mahadev* and Lord *Krishna*.

Now it was time to perform *Antim Sanskar* for *Ajay's* father, family and rest of the villagers.

Bhima looked around, *Ashwathama* was nowhere to be seen.

Ashwathama had reached the *Shiv* temple, in his old cave, where he first started worshiping *Mahadev*, he was crying, crying out loudly, his voice was echoing in the fort, the whole night passed but the crying didn't stopped.

On the other side *Kaali* and *Adhira* flew away with *Achyutanand*, after a day of travel, they reached back to their native place *Mangadu*.

Achyutanand was under surgery, for last three days. *Kaali* recovered from the injuries. *Adhira* and all other were waiting *Achyutanand* to come back to the senses, as per their doctor, he should be in senses anytime.

When *Achyutanand* opened his eyes he saw *Kaali*, *Adhira*, his pregnant wife *Mandakini*.

Achyutanand was still in anger, who brought me here, I wanted to kill that man. *Adhira* said you mean *Ashwathama*.

Ashwathama, Ashwathama... What are you saying *Guru Ji*, was it *Ashwathama,* the fighter of *Mahabharat*, son of *Guru Drona*.

Adhira in tension said, yes, my child it was *Ashwathama,* he was cursed because of me, I influenced him that day when he projected *Brahmastra* on *Uttara's* unborn child, but see *Krishna's* trick, now that cursed *Chiranjeevi* is standing against me.

You are a great warrior, but *Ashwathama* is at different level and now he has got body, body of *Samikshit* and support of *Kaalyogi*.

You are safe after fighting with him, that is big surprise for me.

My 7500 years old *karma,* is standing against me to challenge, I had intuition that *Kaalyogi* will use him someday against me, and that happened now.

We have to be more prepared, before they reach us, and *Adhira* left while saying this.

ॐ पूर्णमदः पूर्णमिदं पूर्णात्पुर्णमुदच्यते
पूर्णश्य पूर्णमादाय पूर्णमेवावशिष्यते ॥
ॐ शान्तिः शान्तिः शान्तिः ॥

Glossary

1972 war	India Pakistan war happened in 1972
Agney Chakr	Energy Chakr on center of eyes
Agni dev	God of fire
Ahamkar	Knowledge of selfness
Anahat Chakr	Energy Chakr on heart
Angvastra	Men's cloth for upper body
Annmay Kosh	Physical body made of food (Ann)
Antim Sanskar	Last rituals after death
Anushtan	Ceremonial process
Ardh Samadhi	Half meditative stage, deep meditation
Arjun	Great warrior of Mahabharat, one of Pandavas
Asana	Posture
Ashtwakra	Guru of King Janak, Father of Sita Ji
Ashwathama	Son of Guru Drona, born with a gemstone on his forehead
AshwathamaMani	A gemstone on forehead of Ashwathama from his birth
Atm-Shuddhi	Self cleansing
Atma	soul
Belpatra	A kind of leave, Lord Shiv loves
Bhagwan	God
Bhadrapada Maas	Sixth month of Hindu calendar from 23 August to 22 Sep.

Bhima	Powerful Pandava, with Mace
Brahma	Creator of Universe, one of the God of Trinity - Brahma, Vishnu and Mahesh.
Brahmastra	Disastrous weapon in Vedic period.
Buddhi	Brain, mind in subtler aspect
Chaar dham yatra	Religious journey to four main temples
Chillam	Smoke pipe made of clay
Chiranjivi/ Chiranjeevi	Immortal
Chitta	One of the four components of Subtle body, storage of memory over many births
Dandvat pranaam	A form of greetings, by lying down in dorsal in front of guru or god
Dandak Aranyak	Dense forest in South of India
Dharma	Code of conduct confirming to one's duty and nature
Dhatura	Poisonous fruit, Lord Shiv loves it
Dhoti	Men's cloth for lower part of body
Dhrishtdyumn	Son of Raja Drupad, Twin brother of Draupadi, who vowed to Kill guru Drona.
Duryodhana	Eldest son Dhritrashtra and Draupadi out of 101 children
Dvapara Yuga	Third leg of 4 yug cycle, Dvapara came after Treta yug, where Ramayan occurred. Timing of Yugas is a great conflict among various schools of thought in present time.
Ganga	Holy river Ganges, Generates from Gangotri
Ganja	Cannabis
Geeta Press	Oldest and biggest press in Gorakhpur famous for many Hindu literature printing and publishing
Gotra	Clan
Guru	Teacher or Mentor

Guru Dron	Guru of Kauravas and Pandavas
Guru-Pita	Father who is guru as well for the kids
Gurudev	Salutation to Guru
Gurukul	Vedic system of schools
Guruvar	Salutation to Guru
Haridwar	A pious city of Uttarakhand
Hastinapur	Largest country in Aryavrat
Havan	Prayer in front of fire
Ida	Channels of life energy in left side body
Kaliyug	Present Yug, fourth leg of 4 Yug Cycle
Karm	The actions done by any living being, It is said that to every Karm there is a result.
Karan Sharir	Causal body
Karna	Sixth son of Kunti, eldest brother of Pandavas, who never got recognition as Pandavas
Kauravas	100 brothers and 1 sister, Elder Brother Duryodhana, Lineage of Kuru Kingdom and son of Dhritrashtra.
Kshama	Apology
Kuldevta	Deity for the clan
Kulpita	Father of the clan
Kupit atma	Devil Soul
Kurukshetra	Battle field of Mahabharata
Maha karan Sharir	Super causal body
Maha-shivratri	14th day of Lunar month in Feb-Mar
Mahatama	Holy saint
Maha-Yodha	Great warrior
Mahamrityunjay Mantra	A mantra to save lives
Mama	Maternal Uncle
Manipur	Energy Chakr on navel
Mann	A subtle form of mind

Mukt Bhava	A blessing to be free from life and death cycle
Muladhar	Energy Chakr on tail bone area
Naadi	Energy channels in body
Nirmankaya	A subtle form which create gross body whenever needed
Nirvan	Knowns as Moksha or Maha parayan, where the soul is free from life-death cycle
Nirvan Shatkam	A poem written by Adiguru Shankaracharya of non-dualism
Pandavas	5 brothers name Yudhistir, Bhim, Arjun, Nakul and Sehdev, Lineage of Kuru Kingdom, Son of Pandu
Pangat	Sitting on ground in line during feast
Pinda	A rice and sesame ball made to offer to dead ones
Pingla	Energy channels in right side body
Prabhu	God
Pradhan	Head of the Village
Prakritik Dharma	Code of conduct one has to follow for nature
Prarabdh Karm	Amount of deeds allotted to every living organism for one life
Prana energy	Life
Puja	Prayer
Putri	Daughter
Putra	Son
Rashtra Dharma	A code of conduct one has to follow for nation
Rishi Markandey	An ardent Shiv devotee, who saved by Lord Shiv himself from hands of death.
Rishikesh	End of hills coming from Uttrakhand
Rishivar	A salutation to Guru
Sadguru	Real teach

Sadhak	Student devoted for prayer or seeker
Sadhu	Saint
Sahasrar Chakr	Energy Chakr on head
Sahasr sudarshan Chakrs	1000 discs
Samadhi	Highest form of meditation, where the yogi leaves body without any physical harm
Samajik Dharma	A code of conduct one has to follow for society
Sanchit Karm	A warehouse of deeds done by a soul across many lives
Sapt	Seven
Sapt Baan Vidya	Shooting 7 arrows at one time
Shaivait	Shiv devotee
Shambhu	Another name of Lord Shiv
Shatam Sudarshan Chakr	A disc having 100 small discs
Shikha	Pony tail on shaved head of brahmins, where Sahasrar Chakr activates
Shiv Puranas	A literature on Lord Shiv with varied topics
Shiv Chalisa	40 lines prayer for Lord Shiv
Shiv Strotam	Sanskrit hymns for Lord Shiv
Shiv stutis	Prayers for Lord Shiv
Shivling	A Lord Shiv idol
Shraddh	A annual ritual of feast for deceased persons in the family
Sudarshana Chakr	A weapon originated by Lord Vishnu and Lord Krishna
Sugriva	Younger brother of Raavan
Sukshm Sharir	Subtle Body
Sushumna	Energy channels in center of body

Swadishthan	Energy Chakr below navel and above tail bone
Tarpana	Offerings to deads
Tantric	Sorcery
Tehravi	Feast organised to brahmins on 13 day of death of family member
Treta Yuga	Period of Ram and Raavan, second yuga of 4 Yuga cycle
Trishul	Trident
Uttara	Wife of Abhimanyu, and daughter in Law of Arjun and Draupadi. Last hope of Pandav clan to continue their lineage
Vaidya	Practitioner of ayurvedic medicines
Vaishnav	Those who worship lord Vishnu
Vanar Sena	Army of forest dwellers, whose clan symbol is monkey
Vajrasan	A form of sitting in Yoga, with knees on floor
Varanasi	Banaras, also known as Kashi, oldest city of world
Vasudev	Son of Vasu, another name of Lord Krishna
Vish Dhumika	Poisnous gas
Vishuddhi Chakr	Energy Chakr on neck
Yamunotri	One of mini-chardham in Uttarakhand, out of Kedarnath, Badrinath, Gangotri and Yamunotri
Yoga	Old Indian philosophy of advocating physical and mental discipline

About the Author

Himanshu Verma, an Information Technology expert by profession and Environmentalist by heart, lives in Noida, Uttar Pradesh, India, with two daughters (Shikhi and Venuka) and wife Sarika Verma.

Ashwathama is first and major work of literature by him, though wrote two more books out of passion for kids, one on *kids stories* and another on *Mathematics tables*.

He is working on this book since 2016, with passion to write something different for *Ashwathama,* not only a cursed warrior of *Mahabharat,* who is living for 7500 years, though give him a new dimension for his role and raise Indian version of superhero.

Other books by Himanshu Verma, available on Amazon and Notion Press

Old Candies in New Wrapper

Stories with new flavour and twist in old famous stories.

This book will take you in your sweet young days. where stories from Panchtantr, were told many times, by your grandma, grand father, parents and teachers.

Math Tables

This book is dedicated for table lovers. I believe that remembering tables should be part of student's life and it should never go away even beyond student life, Math table is one thing which a student should always keep practicing.

Math Tables from 1-25

Math Tables from 1.25, 2.25 upto 24.25

Math Tables from 1.50, 2.50 upto 24.50

Math Tables from 1.75, 2.75 upto 24.75

अश्वत्थामा - Hindi Edition Coming Soon

www.ingramcontent.com/pod-product-compliance
Lightning Source LLC
LaVergne TN
LVHW041220150826
845673LV00001B/466

* 9 7 9 8 8 9 0 6 7 8 8 0 5 *